Guarding Violet

Margarita Harmon

Contents

Prologue

I had the same childhood as most girls do. Dolls, tea parties, fairy tale bedtime stories. And like most girls, my dad tucked me into bed at night and left me with a kiss on my forehead. He was a busy dad, always in and out of meetings and traveling for work, but he always made time to wish me goodnight.

"Daddy, tell me a story." I called to him as he reached for the doorknob of my bedroom. He paused, shaking his head softly.

"I'm sorry, Lottie, but you know I have work." He ruffled my hair, but I quickly grabbed his hand and pulled as hard as my eight year old arms could manage.

"Please, Daddy? One short story?" I pleaded, poking out my bottom lip. My father grumbled and for a moment, I thought he had become immune to my puppy-eyed face.

"Fine." He chuckled, sitting on the edge of my bed. "Once upon a time, there was a beautiful little princes. She was sweet and caring, and generous and kind. Her father, the King, loved the little princess so much that he made a vow to always protect her. So, every time the King would have to leave for war, he would make sure the princess was guarded and safe from all of the monsters of the world. When the King would return home from his work in the kingdom, the little princess would greet him with big hugs and beautiful paintings that she had made just for him. The King knew that there was nothing more important than his princess, and he would keep his vow until his very last breath, even if it killed him."

"That was a lovely story, Daddy." I kissed his cheek and gave him a big hug like the princess in the story had for the King.

"Goodnight, little princess." He whispered to me. When my father opened the door to leave my bedroom, I watched as he spoke to Brock and Cash, in hushed tones. I never listened in on my father's conversations, I knew that he was as wise and just as a king, giving me no reason to worry.

"Goodnight, Brock," I waved with a smile, "Goodnight, Cash." My eyes began to droop and hover over unconsciousness. Dreams of the King and his little princess danced in my imagination.

"Goodnight, Ms. Violet." They said in unison, shutting my door behind my father. I never knew how quite similarly my life paralleled to the little princess in the story, until I got older. But laying in my bed with a soft pink canopy overhead and two armed guards posted outside of my bedroom door at all times, I was living my version of normality. This is the way it had always been and always would be.

But I was not a princess; I was Violet Maddox.

And my father was not a king; he was Talon Maddox, leader of the largest Mob in New York City.

Chapter 1

P op Pop

Gunshots went of from somewhere in the house and I sprang out of bed. Footsteps drew nearer and nearer to my bedroom door, I ran to the knob and quickly locked it. Cash and Brock will take care of whoever is coming. I waited in silence, the footsteps getting louder and louder until they were right outside the door. My heart beat hard in my chest, the silence becoming too much.

"Brock?" I whispered into the dark, hoping he would hear me through the door. "Cash?" The door knob thrashed violently as someone tried to come in. I thanked myself for being quick to lock it.

"Oh, Ms. Violet, can you come out here for a moment?" Cash said menacingly playfully. I shook my head and slid underneath my bed.

"Please, Ms. Violet, we just want to talk." Brock said, but after a few moments of silence, he pounded against the door. "Open the fucking door, Violet!" I slapped my hand over my mouth to keep from screaming. Where is Dad? They continued to punch and kick the door, and while my door was very secure, they had worked for my family for years and knew its weak spots. I curled myself up into a ball and pulled out my rose gold switchblade I had gotten for my eighteenth birthday. They burst into my room, the door breaking into pieces from under them. This is it, I am going to die.

"Ms. Violet..." Cash called into the empty room. "Come out, come out!" He began to look for me, pulling things from my dresser, my vanity, and stripping my bed of its blankets.

"Cash," Brock said from across the room. "Look at these." Their footsteps neared each other and I heard them laugh together.

"I bet Boss doesn't know about these skimpy little black panties you've got in here, Ms. Violet. Why don't you try them on for us-" I heard a gun cock and suddenly the two men I had trust with my life for the past eighteen years gasped.

"Violet, are you okay?" I heard my father call. I scrambled from beneath the bed and ran into his side, holding onto him tightly. He held an MG5 up to them, a deep hatred set into his expression. "You sons of bitches. I trusted you, more than all of the others, with the safety of my daughter. We've worked together for twenty years, you're practically family."

"The new boss offered more money, it's nothing personal Talon. Just business." Cash said, his voice trembling.

"A slip of judgement." Brock took a step forward and my father did the same before screaming in rage and shoving the gun against Brock's temple.

"A slip of judgement, huh? I don't give a fuck about your judgement." My father pulled the trigger, a burst of blood and human matter splatter the wall and carpet. He wiped blood away from his forehead and smiled cheekily at Cash.

"Cash," My father beamed, "Cash, Cash, Cash. What shall I do with you?" He circled around Cash like a predator. "Let you live and send a message to your new boss? Or just kill you? Both send a message and one is obviously favorable over the other." Dad placed his index finger to his lips in deliberation. "I really enjoyed the part where you were talking about my daughter trying on her underwear in front of you. That was my favorite." My father began to tremble with anger, which I knew was a sign he wasn't in the mood for mercy. "Goodbye, Cash. It was good working with you." In the next moment, Cash's brain was sprayed across the wall behind his lifeless body. Several of my parent's guards came in to remove the bodies while my dad brought me to the kitchen where my mother and brothers were taking refuge. My mother and father argued about what to do, where to go, and how to get back at whoever had attempted this attack. One of the on-call chefs made us hot chocolate, and my brothers and I drank it down quickly to avoid listening in on our parents.

Vincent was the oldest of all of us. At the age of twenty-five, he was first in line to take over the family when my father retires. Viktor was second eldest and practically a mirror of a younger version of my father. Vaughn was third in our sibling timeline and has the shortest temper. Then there's Valen, the idiot I had shared a womb with.

"I know what they're going to do." Valen stated, slurping up a soggy marshmallow. I shook, my mouth unable to verbalize my thoughts. "Dad's going to spread us out. Mom will go to the house in Beverly Hills; Dad, Vince, Vik, Vaughn, and me will stay here to plan revenge; and you will go to the Hale's."

"The Hale's?" I wondered aloud, taking another sip of my drink. The liquid burned my throat, but it was much more comfortable than what I was feeling inside.

"Yeah, they're an ally we have in Chicago." Vik shrugged nonchalantly, licking his spoon of the excess chocolate.

"Why can't we go somewhere together? Why do I get stuck with strangers?" I looked back at my father who had his head in his hands, my mother rubbed his back gently to comfort him.

"If we went somewhere together, it'd be too dangerous. We're targets for all of Dad's enemies. If we're all in one spot, like we were tonight, it'd be like killing two with one stone. But instead of two birds, it'd be five." Vincent sighed, running his fingers down his face exhaustively. Valen pulled me into a side hug and squeezed me.

"It's going to be okay, Vi. Dad won't let anything happen to you."

"And what about you guys?" I frowned, hating the way everyone treats me like I'm breakable. "You guys are his kids, too."

"Yes, but you're our baby sister, and Dad's only daughter. We just want to keep you safe." Vaughn knocked my shoulder with his playfully, but I still didn't think it was fair. My father eventually stood and approached us once again. His face held a grave expression that made my heart know that what Valen had said was true. We were going to separate.

"Your mother and I have decided that for everyone's safety, I will stay here and your mother will be going to the house in California. The boys will stay with me. And Violet," His eyes found mine and I could tell it broke him to finish his sentence, "You will be going to Chicago."

The next hour was filled with packing. I wanted my father to see that I was being strong, so I refused to cry. I could cry in the car. My mother pulled me into an embrace, her soft cherry blossom perfume comforted me for a single moment before I remembered we were separating, for who knows how long.

"I love you," She said as she kissed the hair on top of my head. "Please be safe."

"I will." I bit my lip to stop a sob that attempted to rack my chest. We watched as her car drove away and disappeared behind the treeline. It was my turn. All four boys pulled me into a tight group hug, making me laugh for the first time that day. Valen waited until the other brothers had gone inside the house to show he was upset.

"I'm going to miss you," He kissed my cheek. "I'll see you soon, Vi. It's a twin thing, just trust me." My hardest goodbye was saved for last. I turned to find my father leaning against the brick of our upstate New York house, my childhood home.

"The Hale's are good people, strong people. They'll take care of you." He pulled me into his chest and I hug him tightly. I made a point to remember his familiar smell of cigars and sandalwood. "As soon as things clear up over here, I'll come and get you."

"Okay." I whispered softly, knowing he'd keep his word.

"I promise." He croaked, kissing my forehead. Without another word, I slipped into the back of my car and told my drive it was okay to go. I watched as my father disappeared from my view and I finally allowed myself to break down. Everything will be okay, Vi. Everything will be okay.

Chapter 2

I woke up that night to my driver shaking me awake.

"Ms. Violet, we've arrived." He said quietly, helping me out of the Cadillac. I looked around, seeing the tall buildings and bustling streets reminded me of home.

"That was fast drive." I laughed halfheartedly, trying to take in my surroundings. A cement brick building with cast iron cages around the windows, a black door with gold trimming and an elegant knocker.

"You've been asleep for twelve hours," The driver chuckled softly, "I pulled over a few times to see if you were still breathing."

"Oh." I replied silently as the driver used the knocker to rap at the door. I took notice of the gold outlined peephole that we were undoubtedly being stared at through. A few moments passed before the door swung open, a man in his early fifties quickly pulled me in and slammed the door shut again. I was patted down and searched before being allowed to enter the remainder of the home.

"Sorry about all of this, ever since we got news from your father about the break in, we've taken security measures to a new level." The man said, walking in front of me as he showed me around, "My name is Alphonse, I am the leader of the Hale family. I have known your father for many years, he is a good man."

"Yes, Sir." I nodded, looking into each room as we passed by. A sitting room with a long luxurious mahogany lined couch with what looked like plush black fabric as cushions. Several bedrooms and bathrooms, a large kitchen with marble counter tops and stainless steel appliances, a music room, a lounge room, and at some point I just stopped keeping track of everything. Finally we came to a dimly lit hall where a single light shown over a soft pink colored door.

"Your father has sent over a generous amount of money to make sure we provide a room in which you are comfortable." He entered in a security code and opened the door. "We have cameras up and down the hallway leading to your door, a security code to open the door, and a pressurized lock to ensure nothing comes in or gets out."

"Out?" I questioned as the door swung open, my stomach knotting slightly at the fact I was under the same amount of security as a murderer in prison.

"For your own safety, I can assure you that nothing your father wouldn't approve of will happen here." He ushered me instead and followed behind me. I gasped softly, taking in the luxury of the bedroom. "This is your living quarters, obviously this is your bedroom. The door to your left is a small painting studio that doubles as a library. To your right is your bathroom with both a walk-in shower and a bathtub to use at your leisure. The door next to your vanity is a walk-in closet. When you are hungry or in need of anything, just come over to this control panel," He nodded toward a box connected to the wall, pointing to a silver button specifically. "Press call and tell Niklaus whatever you need, day or night."

"Niklaus?" I questioned, still admiring the beautiful room. The bed was, of course, gold trimmed, but had a light pink comforter and white pillows. The floor was a dark hardwood with a white faux fur rug that felt soft against my aching feet. The vanity was a pale white with gold accents, the chair just below it was also white and gold, but had a pink cushion. Two nightstand stood on either side of the bed, mirroring the same color scheme of the vanity.

"Yes, Niklaus, my son. He will be in charge of your safety and care while you are staying with us." He smiled warmly and entered the security code into the control panel, opening the door for him to leave. "I do hope that you will feel comfortable here, Violet. Dinner as at six o' clock, we shall reconvene then." Without allowing me another word, he slipped into the hallway and shut the door. The sound of the pressurized locking system shifted and locked me in. I search the room, no windows, no laptop, no cell phone. The only link to the outside word was a landline phone connected by wires to the wall. A small piece of tape ran across the surface of the phone with black writing that said: monitored. I sighed and picked up the small suitcase I was allowed to bring, and placed it on the bed. As I began to unpack, I realized I hadn't brought any clothes. A few picture frames that held pictures of my parents and my brothers, a hairbrush, a locket my father gave me for my sixteenth birthday, and The Great Gatsby.

The more I sat around, the more I began to think about everything; my father, my mother, my brothers, how everyone I love was in danger but I was the most protected. I felt selfish and undeserving. To take my mind off of everything, I looked into the closet and felt a sense of relief in the fact it was full of clothes and shoes for me to wear. Shirts, blouses, pajamas, sweatpants, jeans, athletic wear, dresses, gowns, you name it. I sent a loving thank you to Dad in my mind. I found myself wondering to the studio where I found an easel, paints, an assortment of brushes, and labeled drawers chalked full of other things. The walls that confined the small studio were lined with books and I slid my old dingy copy of Great Gatsby next to the newer version. Exiting the studio library, I wandered into the bathroom where I lavished the sight of the claw legged bathtub and the walk in shower that was built from stone. The shower's door was frosted glass and I found myself smiling for the first time since I had arrived here.

"Frosted glass? Who is going to see me in here?" I snorted sarcastically to myself, "It might as well be clear." Because I had slept for almost half the day already, I decided to put myself to work and find a new book to read. Two seconds in the studio library and I found my perfect suitor: She: A History of Adventure.

I flitted over to the bed and hopped on, wiggling under the covers until I was comfortable. The book opened and my eyes danced across each line with ease. An hour had passed when I heard the beeping of someone pressing in the security code. I quickly scrambled out of the bed and made myself more presentable, fixing my crooked sweatpants and disheveled long sleeve tee. When the door opened, it wasn't Alphonse Hale like I had expected. It was tall man with curly black hair that fell past his jawline, dark brown eyes that watched me with angry intensity, a five o' clock shadow made up of dark facial hair hued across his upper lip, cheeks, and chin. He wore a pair of tight black jeans and a black long sleeve button down shirt that he had pushed the sleeves up to his elbows.

Wowza.

"So you're the Manhattan Princess, huh?" He looked me up and down, scoffing quietly.

"What?" My brow furrowed in confusion. Why was he so angry?

"Your father is the King of New York, you're the Manhattan Princess?" He said, like it was something obvious that I should have known. "Four big brothers, over protective father, spoiled brat." He shrugged matter-of-factly. My blood began to boil.

"Excuse me, but you don't know me at all. I wouldn't just jump to conclusions-"

"I know enough, Princess." He snapped, leaning against the wall.

"Did I do something to you?" I balled my fists at my sides angrily, knowing I was most likely becoming red in the face.

"You have no idea," He laughed sarcastically, "Now get ready for dinner, my father is waiting."

"You're Niklaus Hale?" I questioned in disbelief. If I have to deal with this guy on a daily basis, either he's going to kill me or I'm going to kill him.

"Unfortunately." He grumbled, facing the other way.

Crap.

Chapter 3

After fighting with Niklaus for another fifteen minutes, I finally got dressed in a light pink oversized long sleeved tee and a baby blue tube skirt. Slipping on a pair of white converse, I walked back into the bedroom where Niklaus gave me a once over.

"You're wearing that?" He cocked in eyebrow. I frowned and looked at myself in the mirror of the vanity.

"What? Sorry I don't look like I'm going to a casual funeral." I stuck my tongue out at him and pushed past him, walking out the door. He followed behind me, cursing under his breath about 'babysitting a spoiled child.' I spun around on my heel, "Excuse me, Sir-" I poked his chest with my index finger, "I'm nineteen, not nine and I may be spoiled but I'm thankful for everything I have. I don't know what I did to offend you, but I do not deserve this!" I folded my arms across my chest. He was quiet for a moment before he slammed me against the wall, his warm breath fanned over my lips as he spoke.

"Little girl, do not push me." He laughed manically, "I may be in charge of keeping you safe, but I can make anything look like an accident." He pushed himself off the wall and started back down the hallway. My heart was practically in my mouth, my skin slick with sweat. I waited a few moments before following, making sense of how that had made me feel. Scared, obviously. I was undoubtedly scared. But I couldn't hid the conflicting part of me that yearned to still be pressed against that wall.

Ugh.

When I finally made my way into the dining hall, I found myself at the end of a long black table. Just across was Niklaus, who refused to acknowledge me. Alphonse Hale was already dining on the other end of the table, sitting adjacent to four other men, most likely talking about their next scheme.

"Excuse me, Ms. Maddox," One of the house workers said as she approached me, "What would you like for dinner?" I pondered the thought for a moment and then it came to me.

"Pizza, please." I smiled and settled in my chair, but the house worker stayed.

"I'm sorry, but you want pizza? You can have whatever you like Ms. Maddox, we have a very talented chef on payroll." She said, attempting to sway my choice.

"No, I'm good with a plain cheese pizza- A large cheese pizza." I corrected myself, giddy to finally eat. And for a split moment, I thought I saw Niklaus' mouth twitch into a smile. But before I couldn't confirm the phenomenon, his face had turned back into stone. A chair pulled out from beside me and

I watched as another man sat down. His hair, like Niklaus', was curly and he sported a slight beard.

"Good evening, Ms. Maddox," He nodded toward Niklaus, "Brother." I looked between the two, only finding their hair to be a shared trait. Noticing my confusion, the brother chuckled. "Different mothers; let me introduce myself, I am Niklaus' older brother, Archor."

"Lovely to meet you." I smiled softly, feeling my stomach growl with impatience.

"Hungry?" Archor chuckled, nodding toward the kitchen door. "Just in time it looks like." The house worker placed the large pizza in front of me and I stared down at it in confusion.

"What is this?" I frown, poking the thick crust with a fork. The pizza looked more like a casserole inside an edible bread dish, filled to the brim with red marina sauce and gooey cheese.

"Chicago style pizza, you've never had it?" Archor asked as he ordered his own food.

"No, actually. I am more accustomed to New York style." I divulged, biting my lip as I debated on where to start with this massive meal.

"New York is a nice city, miss it?" Archor said, suddenly succumbing to a stare down with his younger sibling. I looked between them and nodded awkwardly.

"Uh, yes. I do." I replied simply. To avoid any further conversation, I cut into the pizza and stabbed into the dense crust with a fork, and placed it into my mouth. My taste buds and stomach hummed with happiness. I finished the entire ensemble in no time, and yet my stomach flipped at the sound of dessert. "Yes, please!" I smiled thankfully at the house worker worker who offered me a slice of vanilla cake with a thick buttercream frosting. The two men watched me eat, as if I was a starving child.

"Where are you putting all of that?" Archor laughed as people came to collect my plates. I shrugged, a blush coming to my cheeks in embarrassment. "Don't be bashful, Violet. If you're hungry, eat."

"I'm definitely not hungry anymore." I chortled, patting my belly.

"I'd hope not, you ate half the kitchen." Niklaus said mockingly, his arms crossed on this chest as he avoided my glower.

"Dismiss Niklaus, he's just upset because instead of going on jobs, Dad's assigned him to you." He took my hand and kissed it softly, "If it were me in charge of your safety, Ms. Maddox, I would be more than happy to be in your presence." Archor winked.

"Take her." Niklaus spat, standing in his chair and storming out of the room. I rolled my eyes and sighed, how could I stay here when the guy who's supposed to keep me safe hates me? Wasn't that the point of me coming here; to be safe?

"But in all seriousness, you're safe with Klaus. He'll warm up to you in no time." Archor said as his food arrived.

"I don't like him much either, if I'm being completely honest." I crossed my legs from beneath the table and bit the inside of my cheek.

"He a good guy, Violet, just a hard shell to crack." I wasn't sure about that. But I was hoping that, in time, maybe we could tolerate each other. "So about you..."

"What about me?" I played with my fingers in my lap, not wanting to be shut back in that room just yet.

"Got a boyfriend back in New York? Bet he's worried about you." Archor cut into his steak and dipped a piece of it in some kind of cream sauce.

"No boyfriend." I shrugged, being used to answer this question. Archor's eyebrows shot up in surprise.

"Wow, that's hard to believe. You're gorgeous."

"Well, I wasn't really allowed access to boys growing up. My father insists they are trouble."

"Which they are." Archor chuckled, "How'd he manage to keep guys away from you in school?"

"He didn't have to, I was home schooled. Private tutor." I clicked my tongue against the roof of my mouth and nodded matter-of-factly.

"Pretty protective, I guess."

"I'm the only daughter, my brothers are just as crazy about keeping me safe, hence why I'm here."

"Okay, so let me get this straight. No public school, no boyfriend. So does that mean..."

"Yeah, I've never been kissed." I nod slowly, but this was my normal. I figured I'd date when my dad dies, it'd be easier than introducing him to a boy I like.

"I meant sex, but I guess the two go hand-in-hand. Damn." He laughed quietly and shook his head. "I feel bad for the guy who gets in your pants for the first time." And quite honestly, me too. Another worker bustled into the dining hall with her hand pressed against the receiver of a telephone.

"Ms. Maddox, it's your mother."

Chapter 4

I was escorted back to my room for privacy. Yearning for a voice of familiarity, my stomach twisted in excitement. Once in my bedroom, Niklaus slammed the air-tight door shut. The landline blinked red, indicating a waiting call. I picked up the receiver and placed it against my ear.

"Mama?" I called into the silence.

"Violet." She audibly gasped into the phone, relief flooding her voice. "I'm just calling to check in, did you make it to Chicago alright?"

"Yes, I'm fine. And you?" I savored the sound of her soft voice, her every word lulling my anxieties, even for just a moment.

"I'm okay, considering." There was a pause and I knew what such pause meant. She missed my father and worried for his safety, and the safety of her sons. "I'm just so happy you're okay. How are the Hale's treating you, my dear?" I pondered the question for a moment. "Lottie-"

"I'm fine, it's fine. They're... fine." I nodded, fully aware she could see through the facade.

"One call to Daddy would fix whatever you need right up, you know that right, Sweetheart?" My mother said soothingly, to which I shook my head and sighed.

"I'm okay, Mom, truly. It's just... a change." I mumbled, looking around the lavish room my father had put together for me.

"I know, but don't get used to it. Your father said we wouldn't be here long." She said, a twinge of hope ringing in her saddened voice.

"Yes, Mama." I smiled slightly and twirled the telephone cord around my finger.

"I must be going now, Lottie. Stay well, I'll be checking in again soon." She promised, her goodbye already striking a fleet of fear through me.

"Mama, please don't go-"

"I must, we've already been talking too long. Until we know who is behind this, we need to keep our conversations short and sweet. I love you, we'll talk soon."

"Mom-" The line went dead and I sunk down the corner of my bed, the phone falling from my fingertips in defeat. I was alone; alone for the first time in my entire life. Without my mother, without my brothers, and without my father. Tears fell down my cheeks in waves of sorrow. Before long, my eyelids became heavy from a combination of crying and exhaustion. I hung up the phone, tired of hearing the buzzing noise coming from the receiver, but stayed in my spot slumped against the frame of the bed.

Niklaus

"She's been in there for hours." Archor said, pointing the the door of the brat's room. I rolled my eyes, leaning against the door in a signification of my lack of care. My brother had always been the more warmhearted between the two of us, but for the life of me, I couldn't understand his interest in the fire-haired Barbie in there.

"Why are you so worried? She can't get out and no one can get in; perfect set up." I shrugged, popping an M&M into my mouth.

"At least go and check on the girl." Archor pulled out his pack of cigarettes and placed it between his lips before lighting it quickly with a lighter. "This is your job, little brother, and I can't say it's not a good set up. Poor Nik has to look after a gorgeous redhead while the rest of us are out hustling."

"I'd rather be out hustling." I grumbled, typing in the pass code for the brat's room. Archor flipped me off and began back down the hallway. As the door opened, I pushed it forward and slid inside, keeping my back against the wall as I closed it behind me. My eyes scanned the dark room, looking for any sign of the little menace. Flicking on the lights, I found sight of her bright hair in contrast to the light colors of her bed set that had been sent in from Italy. My shoes clicked against the floor as I made my way over to her, her small frame slumped against the hardwood of the bed. Crouching down to her eye level, I observed her slumbered state. The gentle rise and lowering of her chest, the way her eyelashes fluttered in the REM cycle of her sleep, her galaxy of freckles that peppered her cheeks. A piece of red hair had fallen across her face and I reached out to move it, my fingertips grazing the supple skin of her jawline just as her eyes began to open.

"What are you doing?" She mumbled sleepily, her hand coming out to move the strands of hair herself.

"I was trying to wake you up." I shook her shoulders. "You're welcome." Standing and turning away from her, I shut my eyes to control the beads of sweat that had accumulated on my forehead in embarrassment.

"Why were you trying to wake me up?" She questioned, standing slowly, a pained look on her face.

"Because," I said slowly. "It'd be just my luck for you to wake up in the morning with a fucked up back because you slept weird. I'm not going to take my father's bullshit because you're negligent." Turning back to face her, I placed one arm behind her back and one arm under her legs, scooping her tiny stature into my arms and tossing her across the mattress. She gaped up at me and I rolled my eyes, walking to the other side of the room before flicking the lights off and opening the door to leave.

"Goodnight." She called faintly to me, her small voice barely reaching my ears. Without a word, I stepped out of her bedroom and sealed the door shut.

Chapter 5

"Wake up." A husky voice ordered, shoving me in my sleep to awaken. I groaned softly, removing my tousled red hair from my face. My eyes peeled open, having been glued shut from sleep, to see Niklaus sifting through my closet. A questioning expression followed him as he attempted to create an ensemble that matched. Catching my eye, he threw me a dirty look.

"You can't sleep all day, it's time to get your ass out of bed." Niklaus shrugged passively. "Besides, you'll rot in here if you don't move a little, and how would that look to my father? I plan to take over one day." I sat up on my elbows and watched him pull out a pair of navy blue sweatpants and a white tee; I frowned. "What?"

"I'm guessing we're not going out today?" I said, forming my statement as a question that I already knew the answer to. I was in a luxury style prison, no escape.

"Are you stupid?" Niklaus laughed, checking through the dresser drawers. "My father would sooner shoot me between the eyes than let you roam city."

"I don't see the harm if you're with me." I shrugged softly, stretching my limbs as far as they could bend. Niklaus' eyes flickered to the sleeve of my shirt that had dipped down my shoulder as I moved, and back to my face.

"I'm not about to be your shopping partner, Princess." He grunted, shoving garments around in the drawer.

"I don't want to shop, I want to see the city. I've never been here before." I explained, eyeing his intentions. "I can get myself undie-" Before I could finish, Niklaus pulled out a pair of classic white cotton briefs.

"What the hell is this?" He bit his lip to hold back laughter. Embarrassment flushed my face and I slid out of bed, ripping the undies from his hand.

"My father packed for me, what can I say?" I mumbled, throwing the undergarment back into the drawer and slamming it shut. "Now can we go sightseeing or not?"

"Wow," I marveled at the city below, glancing back at Niklaus who stood disinterestedly against the wall of the Willis Tower. "It's so beautiful." Even though it was a week day, the tourist attraction was packed with couples and families waiting to view the city's horizon. Once I had my fill, I found my way away from the crowd and rejoined my bodyguard. His eyes guarded by the black Ray Bans he was so fond of, made it hard for me to read his expression, but you can't hide that much disdain behind a pair of sunglasses. Without a word, he pushed away from the wall and headed toward the elevator, pressing the button until it lit up and dinged, indicating it was ready to board. The ride down was silent, my ears popping like they had on the way up.

"Now what." He sighed, his fingers dragging through his unruly curls.

"I don't know, tour guide, where to next?" I asked, trying to stay optimistic. Remember what Archor told you, he's better once you get to know him.

"So now I'm your tour guide in this little game?" He cocked an eyebrow from below his Ray Bans. I shrugged slightly, offering a small smile. "Navy Pier, I guess?" I clapped excitedly, appreciatively. Niklaus haled a cab and opening the door, he ushered me to slip inside first. With a sheepish 'thank you,' I slipped inside the cab. After a silent ten minute ride, we arrived at the pier where I looked out over the water. Chicago was a lot slower than New York, quieter than New York. But the pier made me think of home and my heart clenched at the though. It had been a week since I had last spoken to my father and brothers. Noticing a shift in my demeanor, Niklaus motioned toward the Ferris Wheel. "Want to?" I nodded eagerly and boarded the carnival ride with excitement as Niklaus paid. We sat across from each other, again in silence, while the ride went round. My eyes followed the skyline, watching as the afternoon sun faded into a gradient of orange, pink, and red. Suddenly, the Ferris Wheel jerked, sending me across the ride into Niklaus' lap. His large hands gripped my waist protectively as his eyes searched me for injury.

"I'm fine, I'm fine." I promised, nodding my head to reassure him. He flicked his sunglasses atop his head and placed me onto his seat before standing to view the conductor of whom was struggling to control the machine. Police arrived to the scene and communicated to all the riders that there was a malfunction with the mechanism that pushes the Ferris Wheel to turn. Niklaus groaned and sat across from me again, his head in his hands as we waited for the technician to fix the mechanism. "What's your favorite color?"

"What?" Niklaus looked up from his distraught sitting position.

"Well, I figured to pass the time, maybe we could get to know-"

"No, absolutely not. Let's keep this professional, shall we, Princess?" He shot me a fake smile and returned his head to his hands in self-pity. I huffed, crossing my arms over my chest.

"Then call me by my name; my name is Violet." I grumbled, crossing my legs.

"I'm well aware of your name, Sweetheart. Princess just suits you so much better." He mocked, flicking his sunglasses back over his eyes to avoid my angry stare.

"Well, I have a name for you, too, as-" I was cut off by the ride jerking once more, this time giving me enough time to grip the seat to stay steady. Niklaus chuckled lowly and as our ride came to a stop, I avoided the hand he offered as help out of the capsule. Instead of taking a cab and enduring yet another silent car ride, I opted for walking back to Hale Manor. Niklaus followed a couple paces behind me, enjoying the fact he had frazzled me again. Upon seeing me through the peephole, I was allowed inside where I crossed paths with Archor.

"Walk me to my room?" I asked pleadingly, my hands clenched in fists at my sides due to his brother's ass-hole-iness.

"Sure thing, Doll Face." Archor wrapped an arm around my shoulders and pulled me under his wing, leading the way to my bedroom. I could feel Niklaus' stare on the back of my head but I did and said nothing. I was done being nice.

Chapter 6

K laus

"I don't know what you did or said to that girl, but she hates you, man." Archor cackled as he left Violet's room, sealing the door shut. I rolled my eyes, shoving my hands in my pockets as I retreated back down the hallway. "Oh, little brother, wait up for me." Archor jogged to my side, slapping an arm around my shoulders in a way that made my leather jacket make a smacking sound. "You couldn't just try playing nice?"

"She's a brat." I shrugged, my jaw clenched beneath my cheek.

"More like, Niklaus is a brat and is projecting his daddy issues onto a poor, sweet virgin." I stopped walking as Archor emphasized the last word, a wicked smile creeping across his face. "Yes, little brother, we've got a little play thing right here in Hale Manor. I don't know about you, but virgin and red head have been on my list for years. I figure, why not kill two birds with one stone, you know?"

"You're sick." I shook my head, continuing my walk back to my bedroom. Archor continued to follow me, his pace matching mine as I attempted to move faster. "And besides, no guy in their right fucking mind would try taking Talon Maddox's daughter's virginity. That's a suicide mission." Archor took a moment to think about it.

"I'm willing to take that chance." He shrugged, leaning against the wall nearest my bedroom door. "And little brother, thank you so much for being a dick to her. Because while you're doing that, you're driving her right into my bed. Keep up the good work." He patted my shoulder once more before disappearing around the corner. Twisting the handle, I entered my bedroom and threw my jacket across my desk chair, falling into my mattress like dead weight. My eyelids became heavy and drooped over the majority of my line of sight. Shrugging my shirt and jeans off, I slid under the covers of my bed and allowed my eyes to fully drift shut.

The sun drifted through the four windows of my bedroom, as the morning blossomed into full effect, I slid out of bed and stretched my limbs as far as they could go. Slipping into a pair of basketball shorts, I grabbed my headphones from my dresser and jogged out of my bedroom, firmly closing the door behind me. My eyes couldn't help but stare down the ill lit hallway that led down to Violet's bedroom. Visions of her red hair strewn across her pillows danced across my brain before I shook them away. But without realizing, my thoughts grew deeper, imagining the big brown eyes that watched me with hatred and anger. The thought made me smile. Her lips, the way they scowled in the presence; the way they trembled when I pressed her against the wall that first day we met; how they produced my name in such a fucking innocent manner. Without realizing, I had come to a stop, staring down the hallway at Violet's bedroom door like a hawk while thinking about her lips.

What the fuck.

The sudden realization hit me like a train and I was taken aback by my own thoughts. Did I find Violet attractive? Objectively, fuck yes. The thought of bending the mouthy redhead over my desk and fucking her into oblivion no doubt made me hard. But she had a smart mouth that made me want to lock her in her bedroom with a couple boxes of granola bars and a few jugs of water until this assignment was over. She was stubborn and I hated it. She was spoiled and entitled, and I hated that too. Coming to the conclusion that I hated her more than desired her relieved me slightly. Stuffing my headphones on, I opened the door of the house jogged into the street. Like every morning, I avoided the clutter of vehicles and people by jogging down alleyways, climbing buildings and jumping from one to another. After an hour, I headed back toward home. When I was almost three blocks away, a black Cadillac pulled up beside me, throwing a black envelope my way before driving off. I cautiously picked up the paper, noticing the silver wax seal that resembled a C.

Coleman's.

Without opening the elegant paper, I sprinted the rest of the way home, whipping the door open to my father's office without knocking.

"Niklaus, what the fuc-"

"Someone pulled up in a Cadillac, threw this at me, and drove away without saying anything. It's got the Coleman's coat of arms on it." I interrupted him. My father's eyebrows creased as he took the envelope from my hands. Popping the seal, he opened the paper and pulled out a silver invitation.

"On behalf of the Coleman family, the Hale family is cordially invited to the celebration of Sebastian Coleman's birthday." My father read aloud, his eyes reading over the party's details before they widen slightly in surprise. "Handwritten, it says: Please be obliged to bring the daughter of Talon Maddox as well." My heart stilled in my chest.

"How could they know we have her?" I grimaced at the remembrance of our little tour of the city. I should have known the Coleman's would find out. My father set the invitation down and placed his head in his hands, deliberating on what our next move was. Taking a deep breath, his eyes met mine.

"Get Ravon on the phone, we've got to get the girl in for a fitting."

Chapter 7

V iolet

My heart beat hard in my chest, the tight black gown I was sporting not aiding in my need for oxygen, although I appreciated that the sleeves were off-the-shoulder so my skin could easily breathe. My nerves were jumbled in a mess of anxiety. My father never invited me to his work-related events, but here I was: sitting in a black Bentley in an outrageously expensive and lavish gown, not long from being in the home of a rivaling family. I stared out the window, hoping the gently rain that was coming down from the Chicago skyline would alleviate some of my tension.

It didn't.

After a forty minute drive, we arrived at a large white mansion with white pillars standing tall to brace the architecture's enormity. The driver pulled around a tear drop shaped driveway that surrounded a large marble water fountain in the middle. The car came to a stop and the driver slid out of the vehicle, opening the door for me and holding his hand out to me to take. Obliging, I took the man's hand and pulled myself out of the car, allowing him to hand me over to Alphonse who crossed our arms in a way that reminded me of my father.

"If you feel, in any way, threatened or otherwise, alert one of our men and they will take you back to Hale Manor at once," Alphonse patted my hand with his opposite one as we walked up the many steps toward the large home. "Do not feel as though you have to stay on my or my sons' behalf." With a gentle nod, I turned my attention forward. The glass doors were opened for us and we entered the main foyer, my eyes were instantly drawn to the beautiful chandeliers that hung from the ceilings, each one composed of lit candlesticks and crystal, giving off a dim but beautiful light to the open concept. The floor tiles were white marble, making the sound of my heels echo over even the music that was being played. Floor-to-ceiling windows covered the four walls that now surrounded us, giving way to the very same beautiful Illinois skyline that I had been infatuated with earlier as the sun was in its last stages of setting. Avoiding the crowds of people bumping and grinding on the dance floor, Alphonse led me to the bar, ordering himself a shot of vodka.

"It's that kind of night, Sir?" I questioned, a playful tone evident in my voice.

"I am afraid so, my dear." Alphonse chuckled softly, his eyes shifting to something behind me. "Ah, here come my boys." I turned to follow his gaze, drinking in the sight of Niklaus suit-clad and cleaned up. His normally disheveled hair was slicked back and well kept, the unruly beard he had once sported was now nicely trimmed and neat, the black suit conforming to his body as though it were made specifically for the purpose of being worn by him.

Niklaus

Ever since receiving the invitation to Bash Coleman's birthday party, I've been on edge waiting for some kind of trap to ensue. Why else invite the snobby little Manhattan princess? With the birthday idiot no where in sight, my eyes made way for the bar where my father was undoubtedly nursing a bottle of vodka to get him through this evening. Archor at my side, we shoulder past guests in our way, not caring if pushed or shoved others to the side. We are Hales, it's in our blood to be assholes. Nearing the bar, I glanced at my watch and noted the time. Nine o' clock.

"Let's be gone by eleven, knowing Bash this party will last until next week." I groaned, my hands clenching and unclenching to relieve tension.

"Oh, come on, little brother," Archor elbowed my side playfully, "Where's the party animal in you?"

"Not here." I grumbled, my eyes finally finding the bar as we approached it.

Fuck.

My eyes first found the slit in her black dress, her milky skin contrasting against the dark fabric like night and day.

Traveling upward, my eyes found the dress to have hugged her figure in the best of ways, accentuating her small waist and pushing up her bust. And again, there was her skin, unmarked and delectable like melted vanilla ice cream. Her collarbones jutted out in a way that made me want to bite them, suck on them. A diamond choker situated itself around her neck, the small stones gleaming in the soft lighting of the ballroom. Her fire-red hair was curled in waves that flowed down her back. I yearned to wrapped it around my knuckles and pull.

"What?" Her voice broke my trance and I realized I was staring, ogling more like. As her lips moved, I took in the sight of her lips painted red, her eyes accented by black wings that pointed sharply toward her temples.

"Nothing." I snapped, feeling caught. She turned away from me and I was thankful that she did. I loved the way she hated me and I wanted it punish her for it. Approaching my father, I said my hellos and nodded toward the acquaintances to our family who were in attendance of the party. Seconds bled into minutes, minutes I had to force myself not to look at her. But as I focused on this, her attention was elsewhere.

"Hey, bro, I think I know the reason behind Bash inviting Violet." Archor mumbled to me, nodding toward the dance floor. I spun on my heel, watching as Violet's hair whirled around as she was lead in a close dance with Sebastian Coleman. My jaw ticked and I took an angry breath. Archor noticed my mood shift and took a step back, but my eyes never left the back of Bash's head. Without thinking, I stalked forward, purposely shoving people out of my way. Bash dipped Violet's body, leaving the majority of her leg exposed through the slit of her dress.

I growled.

Once she came back up, I tapped on Bash's shoulder and he turned, flashing me his playboy toothy grin. I rolled my eyes.

"Klaus, you made it-"

"Beat it, Bash." I placed my hands on Violet's hips, taking his place. With a smug expression on his face, Bash put his hands up in mock surrender, leaving Violet to me. A pianist played slowly in the background, but I heard nothing as I was now forced to look at her angry, embarrassed face.

"What the hell was that?" She questioned, her nose scrunching up in confusion. My body relaxed slightly as I pushed forward to keep up with the rhythm.

"I was saving you." I answered simply, avoiding her eyes by looking over her head.

"Saving me?" She asked quizzically, "Saving me from what? A pleasant conversation and an amazing dance partner?" I scoffed, rolling my eyes at the compliment. "Oh, like you could do better?"

"I can do a lot of things better than Sebastian Coleman," I leaned in to her, my lips gently grazing against the shell of her ear as I spoke. She gasped softly, shutting her goddamn mouth. To prove myself, I extended my arm and with it she went. After savoring a moment of her surprised expression to boost my ego, I twirled her small frame back into my chest, leaving her back against my front. My head fell into the crook of her neck, my nose brushing against her jawline as my knuckles gently traced down her midsection.

"Nik-"

I silenced her by turning the small woman to face me once again, taking her hand and placing it on the base of my neck before situating my hands low on her waist once again.

"Are you enjoying yourself?" I asked, honestly interested in her reply. She looked at me in utter confusion, her eyes searching my face as if this were all some sort of joke.

"Who are you and what have you done with the Niklaus I know and despise?" She cocked an eyebrow at me, the small gesture causing a slight smile to appear on my lips. At this, Violet seemed to ease into the motions I was leading her in, allowing me to move us along with the music in any way I pleased. "Seriously though, what's up with you?"

"Nothing, I just can't stand when Bash is like this." I shrugged, biting the inside of my cheek.

"How do you know him?" She asked slowly, as if she were afraid she had crossed a line. On a normal day, she would have.

"He's my best friend." I replied simply, frowning slightly at her surprise. "Yes, I have friends."

She nodded and attempted to suppress a playful smile, her red bottom lip caught between her teeth. Swallowing thickly at the sight of her lips, my fingers trailed down her dress, finally making contact with her soft skin. I marveled the sparks that flew through my fingers as I trailed down her thigh, grabbing hold of the back of her knee and hiking it to the level of my waist, holding it their as if it had belonged all along. Like putty in my hands, Violet allowed her free leg to gently drag against the floor as I led her through song after song. To bystanders, we probably looked like a couple caught up in an intimate dance, but my intentions were far from cordial courtship.

"Look, I hate to break this up, but Bash is asking for you." Archor tapped on my shoulder and I slowly let Violet's leg drift down my side. Huffing in annoyance, I pulled Violet's hands from behind my neck and placed her in my brother's care. Trudging through the crowd, I headed toward Bash who was in the VIP section of his party. Only Bash Coleman would have a VIP section at his own birthday party. I crossed the velvet rope and approached my best friend since childhood. His eyes gleamed with mischievousness as he waved me over to the leather seat beside him.

"Enjoying yourself, Klaus?" His eyes zeroed in on the ass of a blonde in a short dress who happened to walk by, "How's the little redhead?" Bash winked, taking a sip of champagne from a flute.

"What's the scheme, Bash?" I sighed heavily, my mind else-where.

"No scheme, I saw the two of you out the other day and I found it odd how you neglected to mention you had Talon fucking Maddox's daughter residing in your home." The blonde reappeared and slipped into Bash's lap, straddling him despite my presence.

"I didn't tell you because there's nothing to tell." I avoided looking at the pair who had embarked on a mission of who could swallow who's tongue first. Bash took a small breath, busty-blonde-girl taking the opportunity to kiss down his neck.

"Oh please, your eyes practically burned through my fuck-ing skull when you told me to beat it." He looked toward the dance floor where Archor and Violet were playfully dancing to a more upbeat number. "Are you two-"

"We're not together." I shot out, my jaw locked as I forced the words out.

"-fucking," Bash stared at me, a devilish smirk on his face, "You like her, don't you?"

"I don't."

"Do, too."

"Don't."

"Do, too!"

I pushed myself out of the chair and stalked out of the VIP section. God, I fucking hate him. Shouldering past the guests, I made my way to the balcony that overlooked the city. Because it was nearing winter, no one was outside due to the cold. I leaned against the railing, taking deep breaths in an attempt to calm down. I don't like her. I can barely tolerate her.

"Niklaus?" A small voice called from behind me. I didn't turn, knowing the just who that velvety voice belonged to. After a moment, I heard the soft click of her heels against the marble floor and she placed her hands against the black iron railing. "I saw you come out here and I thought I'd check to see if you're okay."

"I'm fine." I spat, my jaw once again ticking in irritation.

"Are you sure, you looked a little-"

"I said I'm fine, Violet." I snarled, turning away from her. She sighed softly and I heard her turn, taking one step before I caught her wrist. Pulling her into my chest, I looked down at her shocked expression, taking in her confused brown eyes and the slight pout of her lips. Her breathing was sharp, her chest rising and falling quickly. Bringing my free hand up, my fingers traced the outline of her defined cheekbones causing her eyelids to flutter. My heart raced as I watched her beneath me, responded to even the smallest touch. Throwing caution out the fucking window, I pulled her forward and press her lips to mine. A surprised yelp came from her lips, but to my surprise, Violet didn't push away. Her lips melded against mine, the kiss turning hard and angry. My hands slipped down her sides, gripping her hips roughly as hers found my hair, tugging and using my locks to pull herself closer.

Fuck.

Chapter 8

Violet

Vibrant purples, greens, and blues erupted from my paintbrush. I swirled the brush around the paint, mixing gold with periwinkle and smudging the paint along the canvas. My brush hovered over the charcoal black, my mind wandering to the night Niklaus had kissed me. Heat rushed to my cheeks as I touched my fingers to my lips. Out of all people on this planet, I never imagine Niklaus Hale to have been my first kiss. The door to my bedroom opened and closed, and I hollered to whoever entered that I was in the library. The door to my little sanctuary opened and I turned to view the devil himself leaning against my bookshelf. Cocking an eyebrow, I gave my attention back to my painting and attempted to hide the girlish blush that had risen to my face.

"You're uncharacteristically quiet." Niklaus said quietly, his voice husky like he'd been asleep all day.

"You're uncharacteristically not an asshole." I quipped, dabbing the paintbrush as I spoke. Nik's face scrunched up like he bit into a lemon, clearly unhappy with my response.

"Your mom's on the phone."

"Okay." I slipped past him and out of the library. Plopping on the bed, I pulled up the phone and wrapped the cord around my index finger. "Mom?"

"Violet, it's so nice to hear your voice, how are things going?" She asked, her voice sounding the most relax I've heard from her since that night back in New York.

"It's been good, I'm staying safe and what not." I replied, wiping a bit of sweat away from my upper lip.

"How're the Hale's treating my girl?" She smiled into the receiver. My eyes wandered to Niklaus who was watching me through hooded eyes in the doorway of the library.

"Pretty good," I bit my lip and dragged my eyes away from the bipolar man in front of me. My mother continued to inform me that my father had a lead on who had paid my bodyguards to switch teams, but Dad had given her no other information beyond that. We said our goodbyes and I hung up the phone. Sliding off of the bed, I padded back toward the library, nearly clothes-lining myself as Nik put his hand out to block my way in. My heart thumped hard in my chest, feeling like a bug under a microscope as he gazed down at me. Bringing his hand up, his thumb brushed across my lips. Heat scorched across my body, my breathing hard and shallow. Showing me a smudge of blue paint he had recovered from my skin, he turned on his heel and headed toward the door.

"Dinner's at six."

At six o' clock, I left my room in a pair of baby blue joggers and a plain white long sleeved shirt. As I closed my door, Ravon flagged me down to walk him to the dining hall. We talked about the gown he had fitted for me the night of Sebastian's birthday party.

"How's it going with Klaus since, you know," He wiggled his eyebrows at me and I blushed, pushing him playfully.

"I shouldn't have told you," I mumbled, feeling even my ears burn with embarrassment.

"Oh come on girl, after years of knowing uptight Niklaus Hale, it's good to know the guy has thoughts beyond 'steal' and 'kill.'" Ravon and I entered the dining hall and where the entire Hale family greeted us with a polite nod. Feeling Nik's eyes on me, but I avoided eye contact. It had been almost a week since the kiss and besides when he wiped the paint off of my lip, we had avoided almost all contact with each other. He informed me of calls for me and when to be at meals, but otherwise we completely stayed away from each other.

I sat down, folding my hands in my lap as one of the maids asked me what I'd like for dinner. Once I had ordered a bowl of broccoli Alfredo noodles, Ravon ordered a Southwest salad and began talking about an issue of Vogue he had shown me at my fitting. After dinner, Ravon walked me back to my room and kissed my cheek goodnight before I entered my bedroom. I painted for an hour, changing my original painting of cool colors to warm reds, oranges, and yellows. Changing into a big shirt and a pair of panties, I slipped into bed and turned on the nightstand lamp to read. Having fallen asleep a couple hours in reading, the lights of my bedroom flicked on and I squinted under the harsh artificial lighting.

"Violet." Niklaus glowered down at me, closing the door of my bedroom. I rubbed my eyes lazily and yawned, stretching my limbs to wake myself up.

"Is something wrong?" I hummed, swallowing thickly as I must've been sleeping with my mouth open.

"Yes," He sat on the edge of my bed. "We need to talk." I was suddenly very much awake, the color draining from my face. This was the conversation I had been dreading.

"W-What about?" I bit my lip, attempting to feign confusion. He rolled his eyes at me.

"Cut the shit," His jaw ticked, emeyes staring holes into my head. "You know what I'm talking about." Sighing, I nodded softly, not willing to be the first to talk. "I was stupid and it shouldn't have happened." I stayed quiet, picking at my comforter with my fingers. "If I could go back-"

"Why are you here?" I arched an eyebrow, "If you're about to tell me it was stupid, I knew that. If you're about to tell me it's not going to happen again, I know that, too. We're on the same page, Niklaus. Let's just forget it ever happened. You can go back to hating me and vice versa." I shrugged, biting the inside of my cheek.

"Yeah," He mumbled, "Forget it." We sat in silence for a long time. "Fuck you, Violet."

"Excuse me?" I glared at him, shock riddled on my face.

"Fuck you." He stood, heading toward the door. Pulling myself out of bed, I followed behind him, shoving his shoulder as my book made an audible thump against the floor.

"You come in my room, tell me we need to talk about that kiss, and now you're storming off? I don't think so." I snapped, shoving him once against to face me.

"Push me again, Violet, I fucking dare you." He growled, his eyes fired by rage. But I was mad too; angry by the way he was acting, angry at his stupid face. I brought my hands up and pushed him hard in the chest. He didn't budge. His hand came to my throat and he back me into the wall, his grip on my neck gentle but assertive. I audibly gasped, my eyes wide with shock and fear. Waves of anger spilled from him, his breathing hard and aggressive. And all in one instant, his lips were on mine. Instantly melting into the kiss, my hands bunched at his shirt, tugging at the fabric. Removing his hand from my throat, his fingers wrapped around the bottom of my thighs and hoisted me against the wall, wrapping my legs around his waist. Nik's tongue swiped over my bottom lip and I moaned, allowing him to deepen the kiss. His fingers toyed with the hem of my panties, teasing the sensitive skin that had been seen by no other man before. Nik pulled away, gathering my hair in his fist and tugging it to the side to expose my neck, the simple movement causing pain to erupt on my scalp and heat to gather at my core. His lips and tongue assaulted the tender skin of my throat, my fingers lacing in his hair and my hips pressing against his. And all at once, he placed me on my feet like I weighed nothing, pacing back and forth like a madman. "Fuck, Violet, we need to stop doing that."

"I know." I murmured and bit my lip as it felt almost numb, looking at the floor to avoid his eyes. Stalking forward, he grabbed my face in his hand, his thumb pulling my lip from between my teeth.

"Stop biting your lip or I'll fuck you right here, right now." He growled, closing his eyes to restrain himself.

"We can't keep doing this." He hissed through clenched teeth.

"You said that already," I mumbled through tight lips as he continued to hold my cheeks between his fingers. Forcing himself away from me, Nik scowled deeply and started pacing again.

"What do we do?" He huffed, his hair becoming the unruly mess I was accustomed to.

"Self control?" I proposed, cocking an eyebrow at its obviousness. Shooting me a vexed expression, I sealed my lips, allowing him to parade around my room in hysteria.

"I can't control myself around you, Violet. I've tried everything to stop myself; avoiding you, fucking girl after girl to get you out of my head, but goddammit-" Our eyes met and his softened only for a moment before they became hard around the edges once again. "I'm assigned to protect you, any relationship beyond my professional duty to you is inappropriate."

"I agree." I stated, keeping his eye contact.

"So it's settled then," He swallowed thickly and turned on his heel to leave. In that moment, I realized how much power I must have over this psychotic man, how much I must effect him. "Goodnight, Ms. Maddox." He called to me, turning back to face me as he opened the door to let himself out. Bending over so the large shirt came up to reveal my pantie-clad bum, I picked up my book from the floor.

"Goodnight, Niklaus." Standing up to my full height, I placed the book on my nightstand, Nik's wide eyes following my every movement. Climbing onto my bed on all fours, I slid under the covers. "Please turn off lights when you leave." And as if my final comment broke his trance, Niklaus quickly flicked off the lights and slammed the door behind himself.

Chapter 9

The next morning, I got word from Ravon that Alphonse and Archor were leaving for a work-related trip that would last through the next two weeks. Apparently their absence was due to some newly developed information regarding my family's situation, but as usual, I was kept in the dark as far as details were concerned. Half of the Hale's men were going with on this assignment, leaving me to Niklaus and a handful of bodyguards.

After patriarch of the Hale family had left the manor, others followed suit, one after another leaving me alone with the man who's made it his life's concern to ignore me unless I was in some sort of immediate danger. I slipped into a pink blush colored two piece swimsuit with a flannel to cover me up before I tip toed out of my bedroom. Ravon had told me that there was a pool right here in Hale Manor and I made it my goal to take a dip. My small feet padded against the door, my nerves bubbling in hopes I wouldn't come face to face with Nik. I blindly followed the end of the corridor, hoping that by some grace of a higher power, that I would find the pool all on my own. Footprints neared me from the other side of the next corner and my anxieties pushed me to slide into an unlocked room. Quietly shutting the door behind me, I heard the footprints stop in front of the door. Flattening myself against the adjoining wall, I watched as the door opened and the person stepped inside, investigating the room for possible intruders. Covering my mouth to obscure the sound of my breathing, I waited a few beats before I watched as the person shut the door behind them. With a sigh of relief, I waited a minute before discreetly slipping out of the room. After a couple wrong turns, I finally made my way to the chlorine scented room. Pushing through the door, the moisture and humidity of the room hit me and enveloped me, my skin erupting in goosebumps.

Setting the flannel on a lounging chair nearby, I shuffled over to the deep end of the pool, gently dipping my toe inside the cool water. Biting my lip, I took a few steps back and ran for it, plunging into the pool in the most ungraceful way. I pushed upward against the water and surfaced, laughing at my body's shivering in reaction the the water's temperature. Slowly adjusting, I kicked my feet and dove under once again, letting the serene, peacefulness of the liquid surround me. I counted the seconds by, the seconds turning into a minute, a minute turning to two. Suddenly, the water around me shifted and a pair of arms wrapped around my waist, pulling me toward the break of the water. My lungs gasped for air and I rubbed my eyes to rid of the blur.

"What the actual fuck, Violet!" Nik yelled, his hands holding onto me tightly as if I'd melt away. "Has your stay here worsened so much that you'd actually try to drown yourself?"

"I wasn't drowning," I bit my lip to suppress a smile.

"Yeah, thanks to me." He mumbled with a frown, his eyes finally meeting mine. Nik held me for a long time, his hands holding my flush against him in. His curly hair had been flattened by the water, the soft locks sticking the moisture on his face. One of his hands came up and my breath hitched as he cupped my cheek. He leaned in, his nose touching mine intimately as our breath mingled between the mere milometers between our lips. His hand fell from my cheek and caressed the skin of the back of my neck, erecting a moan from my mouth. Nik hummed at the noise in approval, his thigh coming to part mine. Now straddling his leg underwater, I held onto his soaked black shirt. I felt his cupid's bow trail against my bottom lip and I shivered, my core heating at the small touch.

"Swim with me," I whispered, almost inaudibly, pulling away from him slowly. His hands drifted from my hips and he watched me quietly, the water bobbing at my collarbones as I swam. I drifted through the water and laid on my back, closing my eyes softly. A few moments later an arm was beneath me, hovering beneath my weight as another hand's fingers grazed down the nape of my neck, following the natural dips of my body. Nik's fingers softly grazed down my chest plate, slowly moving between the crevice of my breasts and then down my navel. My back arched slightly and Nik's hand was eager to catch this movement.

"So, so beautiful." He murmured, his breathing deep and labored. My eyes slowly opened once again, taking in the sight of Niklaus' hooded eyes, darkened with lust.

"Nik?" I whispered breathy, my body sinking slightly until my feet touched the pool floor. His hand reached for mine and he pulled me into him, my breasts pressing against his chest, my nipples hardening in a combination of being cold and aroused. Water dripped from my hair, dripped from his stubble. I watched the small beads cascade down his throat and onto his shirt. "Nik." I said once more, unable to produce more than his name from my mouth.

"It's so hard not to kiss you," He noted softly, his thumb brushing across my lips in longing. "So hard not to bite your lips," He pinched my bottom lip gently, his jaw ticking. "So hard not to push you against the wall of this pool," He placed his large hand against my navel and pushed me forward, my back meeting with the cold wall; I gasp. "So hard not to dive beneath the water and pull off that pretty little bikini." I whimpered softly, his eyes not leaving mine as he lowered himself to press soft kisses down my chest. "Kiss that lovely pussy of yours." All the air in my lungs jutted out in an instant.

My thighs clenched hungrily and Nik noticed, a sly smirk appearing on his face. "Oh, Ms. Maddox, am I making you wet?" My heart hammered in my chest.

"W-Well, technically I was w-wet before you came in here." I stammered, biting my lip. His smirk deepened and I swallowed thickly.

"My simple touch makes your nipples stiffen, don't think I hadn't noticed, Violet." Nik's tongue wrapped each syllable of my name. "Your breathing, your little fucking moans drive me insane like you wouldn't believe. It takes so much restraint when I'm near you." He pulled my legs and placed them around his waist, burying his face in the crook of my neck. "The way you walk with that little bounce in your step; the way you look at me." He sighs heavily, his lips pressed against my shoulder. "You are insatiable, your purpose of existence is meant to tear me apart, isn't it?"

"Maybe," I smiled against his hair.

"I can't stand you," He groaned quietly against my skin, "And yet I can't stand to be without you."

"I know the feeling," I mumbled softly, my hand brushing down his back.

Chapter 10

Niklaus

I wrapped Violet in a towel and escorted her back to her bedroom where I left her to dry off and change. Escaping to my own bedroom, I quickly slammed the door behind myself and slid down its length. My head felt heavy in my hands as I relived the last half hour over and over in my mind.

What the fuck. What the actual fuck.

"You kissed her, you stupid fuck," I pushed away from the floor and paced around my bedroom. But God, did she taste fucking good- No, fucking amazing. It was like her mouth produced saliva made from strawberries and cream. I peeled out of the wet clothing that stuck to my body like a second skin and slipped into a pair of joggers and a plain white tee. I slid my fingers through my coiled hair and sighed, welling enough confidence within myself to exit my bedroom. I slowly made my way back down her hallway, my nerves swelling to twice their normal size as I imagined her plump, pink lips; her long red hair; those big brown doe eyes. "Stop." I growled to myself as I approached her door. I knocked once before entering Violet's room and my breath hitched at the sight of her.

"Hey," She smiled softly as my eyes shamelessly drank her in. Her long, milky legs were covered by a pair of light grey leggings that conformed to each God. Damn. Curve., especially that of her thick, pert ass. The baby blue tee clung to her upper body as if it depended on it, straining against her bust as if it would burst out. And just as my eyes flitted across her chest, my knees turned weak as her nipples pebbled from beneath the fabric.

"Oh fuck." I whispered, my eyes unable to look away from the delicious sight, my mouth water at the thought of taking the little nubs into my mouth and swirling my tongue around them. I felt my cock harden in my joggers, but I couldn't move. It was like Violet had suddenly shifted into Medusa, and with one look, turned my dick hard as stone.

"Nik?" She looked over me with slight confusion and worry. I shook my head, my teeth taking my bottom lip harshly between them.

"Yeah, hey." I spoke hoarsely, my throat suddenly becoming as dry as the Sahara desert. With a thick swallow, I forced my eyes away from her and drifted to her closet, sifting through her clothes. "Do you only wear pink and light blue?" From my peripheral vision, Violet looked down at herself and shrugged.

"Not necessarily by choice." She sighed and plopped down on her bed, her full chest bouncing slightly with her lack of bra. My cock twitched.

"How's that?" I raised an eyebrow in confusion, still filing through her wardrobe.

"My father has always picked out my clothes." She shrugged again, as if it was normal that a father would still picked out his nineteen year old's clothing. Sighing softly, I turned on my heel and grabbed her wrist, pulling her toward the door. Once in the hallway, I dragged her toward my bedroom. "Where are we going?"

"Shopping, but first, you're changing," I avoided her cheeky gaze. Once in my bedroom, I sat the redhead on my bed and grabbed a pair of dark grey joggers and a baggy black crew neck. Placing the clothing in her lap, I nodded toward my bathroom. "Go change. We leave in five minutes." I reached for her throat, my thumb gently tracing her sharp jawline. "Be quick, Babygirl." Pushing her into the bathroom, her normally milky skin tone had gone completely red as I slammed the door shut; not just to tease her, but to hold myself back. Two minutes later, Violet shyly opened the door and I almost growled at the sight of her in my clothes.

Too fucking cute for her own good.

The drive to the mall was short, as Hale Manor was in the middle of the city. I found a parking spot and slipped away from the car, jogging to the passenger side to open Violet's door. As we entered the mall, I slipped my hand into hers, entwining our fingers to ensure her presence at my side. I felt her eyes on me in response but I said nothing, and I felt as though I didn't have to explain myself. Violet and I made our way through almost every single store. This girl had never been shopping in her life and it showed, as her eyes were wide with wonder and excitement. I let her flit across each store, filing through racks and trying on different items. By the near end of our spree, Violet had racked up eight bags of clothing and four boxes of shoes.

But Violet's eyes had found a store that I was physically unable to will myself to enter with her.

"Victoria's Secret." She tested the name in her mouth and peered through the window. "What kind of stuff do they have?"

"Um," I gnawed at the inside of my cheek, "Stuff like, um, underwear? Bras… Lingerie?" Violet's cheeks reddened and I chuckled. "You're welcome to go inside, but I'm not going with you. I just can't." Violet's bottom lip was pulled between her lip as she deliberated before she nodded and started toward the entrance of the store.

Violet

I entered the store and my eyes widened. Pictures of models in silken underwear, panties, bras, and lingerie hung on the walls. My fingers trailed across the soft fabrics and bit my lip harder, not knowing one bit about any of this stuff. I felt a presence behind me and shifted to see the person, smiling politely at the saleswoman who offered me a basket for my possible findings.

"Hi there, welcome to Victoria's Secret," Her eyes looked over me and laughed softly, "Is this your first time in the store?" I blushed.

"Is it that obvious?" I chuckled, embarrassed.

"No, Sweetie, you just seem lost. Do you know your sizes?" She questioned, pulling open some drawers to offer me different types of panties.

"Well, I know my... underwear are medium, but I don't know my bra size outside of sports bras." I blushed again, embarrassed by the fact I am nineteen and unknowing of my own bra size.

"Oh, Sweetheart, we can fit you right here in store. Would you be interested in that?" She asked, her name tag reading the name Rita. I nodded eagerly and followed the woman to the fitting rooms. She measured my chest and wrote down my size: 36D. "I would've never guessed there was so much under that baggy shirt." Rita teased with a wink and I laughed, shrugging my shoulders.

"Not my choice in outfit." Rita nodded knowingly.

"Was it the choice of the curly haired hunk that was watching you from outside the store?" She cocked an eyebrow in question and I blushed in response. "I see." She nodded cheekily. "Boyfriend?"

"NO- No." I shook my head and took a deep breath, "I mean... I don't know." I sighed, my mind falling in the never-ending pit that was Niklaus. Rita threw her head back in laughter and squeezed my shoulder reassuringly.

"How about this?" She eyed me evilly. "We put something together that will make him never want to let you go." She walked toward a rack of black lingerie. "He seems like the type to enjoy the color black."

"He is." I nodded, my eyes searching the room for Nik to avoid complete embarrassment. Rita pulled out black satin ensemble with matching garters and faux diamond trim-mings.

"How about this one? It would really make your hair pop." She winked and I blushed for the millionth time, nodding quickly. Yes, that was the one.

Chapter 11

The phone on my nightstand rang as I was putting my new clothes away. I had separated things by color, now that my wardrobe no longer exclusively consisted of light blues, pinks, and purples. My closet now looked like that of a rainbow and I took a step back to smile at the sight. When I finally registered the phone ringing, I scrambled to collect the call before it dropped. Picking up the landline, I pressed it against my ear and splayed across my soft, generous bed.

"Hello?" I called into the receiver, my stomach twisting with excitement having not heard from any of my family for awhile.

"What took you so long to answer?" My twin's voice sounded and I rolled my eyes, a smile sprouting on my lips.

"I had to stomach the fact I'd be talking to you," I teased, rolling onto my back, "How's home?"

"Good, I guess. Dad's running himself mad trying to find the guy who did this-"

"It could've been a woman, Val." I suggested, picking at my cuticles as I spoke. Valen audibly scoffed and I could practically see him roll his eyes.

"Yeah, okay." He paused for a moment. "How're the Hale's treating you?"

"Um," I bit my lip, thoughts of Niklaus' lips clouding my vision. My hands in his hair, his hands on my throat...

"Violet?" Val pressed, assuming my silence to be cause for concern, "If they hurt you in any way-"

"Oh my gosh, I'm fine, I'm fine; I promise." I insisted, "I just spaced out for a second there." He let out a sigh of relief and chuckled.

"Alright, cool. You scared me for a second there, Vi. So how do you occupy your princess ass? I hear Dad's orders were to have you on complete lock down." Voices sounded in the background and there was a struggle on Val's end of the call. "Get the fuck off, Vinny, she doesn't want to talk to you-"

"Hey Baby Sis, we miss you over here, are any of those Hale guys messing with you? One word and I'll kick some serious ass-" More struggling from my brothers' side of phone and I rolled my eyes, a wide smile on my face. I miss them.

"Little sister! It's been so different around here without you, have you tried any Chicago-style pizza? I heard that shit's crazy good-" Vaughn voice boomed through the phone before Vik made his appearance.

"Seriously Vi, you've got to get back here quick. I can only tolerate so much of these idiots; there's got to be an even balance of rational and irrational around here, and with you gone, the irrational is definitely outweighing its counterpart." He spoke quickly, knowing his time with the phone was dwindling before Valen reclaimed it.

"Sorry about that, we're all going nuts without you and Mom around." Val chuckled, his voice a mixture of bitter-sweetness.

"How is Dad...?" I didn't know how to finish my sentence. Having not called me in all the time I'd spent at the Hale's, he must still fear I am in danger. Not being able to even hear his voice was painful all in itself.

"Do you want the real answer or a lie?" Valen question, his tone suddenly icy.

"The real answer," I said softly, my heart rocketing with fearful anticipation. Valen sighed and I could imagine him running his hands through our identical bright red hair.

"He's awful, hasn't slept in days. If he's not bat shit nuts, he's bat shit angry. The other day he was talking about stringing whoever did this up by their dick and watching as their body weight eventually rips it off." I grimaced involuntarily, the thought of my father doing that to anyone made my blood run cold.

"This is all my fault, I'm so sorry you guys-" I felt my eyes well, the weight of my father's well being and my brother's being overworked trying to find whoever had a hit out on me was constricting my lungs. I couldn't breathe.

"No," They said in unison, their deep voices easing the ton of bricks I felt on my shoulders.

"None of this is your fault. You were born into a family legacy that has enemies. Whoever did this to you has to pay. No one fucks with the Maddox's; no one." Vinny's voice seethed, my imagination pictured his fists balled, knuckles white with fury.

"Don't you worry, Little Sister. We're bringing you home soon, that's a promise." Vik promised, his words making my heart expand to twice its size. We said our goodbyes and I hung up the phone. I laid on my bed for awhile, thinking about my brothers and my father, and how all of this had started. I hadn't realized so much time had passed until a hard, curt knock on my door sounded and Niklaus filed through my bedroom door.

"Hey," He smiled warmly, stuffing his hands into the pockets of his sweatpants. "I excused the chefs and waitstaff for the day, but we haven't eaten dinner yet. Any requests?" The thought of Nik cooking me food lifted my sad little heart a little. I pushed myself off of the bed and jogged the distance between us, flinging my small stature into his large one. My arms wound around his muscled abdomen and pulled him into a tight embrace. His cologne caused my head to spin, my cheek pressing against the soft fabric of his cotton tee. Nik stood statue-like for a moment, his body stiff and obviously confused at my affectionate action. But after a few moments, his muscles relaxed and his arms wrapped around my back, his fingers traced soothing patterns down my spine. I pulled away slowly and headed toward the door that led into the hallway. Nik was hot on my trail, his presence directly behind me as I made my way to the kitchen. "...What was that about?"

"I needed a hug." I shrugged, pushing through the kitchen doors. The kitchen itself was, of course, immaculate. The counter tops were a grey and black marble, the cabinets white with black trimming, all electronics and appliances were stainless steel and brand new. Opening the fridge, I skimmed through everything in stock and pulled out everything I needed. Nik watched me silently, but his stare didn't bother me right now, I was too deep in thought to care about his prying eyes. Putting a large pot of potatoes and water on the stove, I started by peeled and cubing a few carrots before sauteing them in olive oil until they became tender. Adding in a cut up onion, I stirred the mixture until that too became beautiful caramelized, finally throwing in a hunk of ground beef. Sifting through the herb drawer, I found the appropriate seasonings and added them to the beef and vegetables. Niklaus was at my side suddenly, his hands working at his own creation as we cooked in a comfortable silence.

When the beef was thoroughly cooked, I drained it of its fat and, added a fair amount of butter and peas. Throwing in a sprinkle of flour, I stirred my concoction and hummed at the beautiful aroma. The scent of the traditional dish bringing me back home to my mother's kitchen. With a shot of wine, tomato paste, and Worcestershire sauce, I reduced the heat of the stove and added some chicken stock. A few minutes on a low temperature allowed the mixture to become a thick meaty gravy-like substance. I greased up a glass casserole dish with butter and slid the mixture from the pan to the dish. I pulled the boiling potatoes from the stove and drained the water, the meat of the potatoes sliding out from the skin easily. Adding cream, milk, and butter, I mashed the potatoes until they were thick and creamy. Using a piping bag, I piped the potatoes on top of the meat and vegetable mixture and painted the mashed potato topping with melted butter. With a jut of finality, I slid the dish into the oven and let it back to a golden perfection. Nik and I set the table for two. Two place settings, two wine glasses, two sets of cutlery, and so on. When I brought out the Shepherd's Pie, Niklaus' eyes bulged and I smiled in satisfaction. I cut him a slice and slid it onto the white china.

"Oh my god," He moaned out between forkfuls, "This is so fucking good. How'd you learn to cook like that?"

"My mother taught me," I mused with a smile, eating my own slice of pie with vigor. Nik let out another moan and I couldn't help but giggle, earning a coy smile from the devil himself.

"You know, I had no intention on you cooking tonight. I had planned on making us some pretty exquisite Kraft macaroni; however, I do have a special surprise in store for us this evening." He added another slice of pie to his plate and I nodded in mock seriousness.

"I'm so sorry to mess up your plan, next time, the kitchen's all yours." I saluted him and he rolled his eyes, quickly finishing his second piece before grabbing our plates and disappearing to the kitchen once again. I folded my hands in my lap in anticipation for Nik's special surprise he had waiting for me. He reappeared with a silver cake stand with a matching top that hid his surprise from my sight. Setting the stand on the table, he winked at me before grabbing the top and exposing a thick, golden cake with slices of strawberries circling the top.

"Wow," I grinned widely, "Can I keep you?" Nik rolled his eyes again and sliced us both a piece of cake, showing off it's many layers of both cake and icing.

"It's an eight-layer Honey Cake; just like your mom, my mom taught me this recipe." He gave a slight shrug and a moment of sadness crossed his face before he replaced it with indifference. Not wanting to push him, I sunk my fork into the dense cake and shoveled it into my mouth, a moan escaping my own throat at the delicacy. Niklaus' eyes suddenly darkened, the air in the dining hall suddenly thick and barely breathable. I quietly finished the piece of cake and thanked him for making it for me. "I'll walk you back."

The walk back to my bedroom was made in silence. The only sound reverberating from the walls were the sounds of the pads of our feet meeting the floor with each step. When we came to the steel door that was the entrance to my room, Nik's large hands were suddenly on my hips, pressing me firmly against the wall, caging me between it and his body. One of his hands came up my trace the length of my jawline before his thumb and forefinger pulled my bottom lip between them. The pad of his thumb traced along the soft, sensitive skin before letting it fall back in its place against my teeth. Nik leaned in ever so slowly, his lips flirting with mine for a moment, just barely grazing my skin before pressing them firmly against me. But this kiss was somehow different than the others we had shared before, this kiss was soft and slow, sensual and affectionate. I could taste the honey and icing on his lips, the sweetness consuming my mind and adding fuel to my incinerated core. Nik sucked softly on my bottom lip before pulling away, his hands still on my face as he pressed one final kiss to my forehead.

"Goodnight, Violet." He murmured before pushing away from the wall and turning down the hallway.

Chapter 12

A week went by with little connection to Niklaus. He took his meals in his bedroom and spent most of his time weight lifting in the Hale's indoor gym. I occupied myself painting, reading, and swimming for an hour a day. Ravon stopped in my bedroom most afternoons to go over fashion magazines and gossip about which guards were cute. On Friday night, Ravon popped his head into my bedroom for the fifth time this week, swinging a movie around in his rich, ebony hands.

"Silent Hill, ever seen it?" He questioned, wiggling his eyebrows and plopping onto my bed next to me. When I shook my head, he gasped dramatically. "But it's only the best movie. It's like Little House on The Prairie, but it's based around a mute girl. Beautiful film."

"I've never heard of it." I said aloud, looking at the DVD through the clear casing it was within.

"Wanna watch it?" He grinned, his eyes squinting with the intensity of his smile. With a smile and a nod, I stood and started for the door. "Wait!" I turned to face him with a questioning expression. "Let's make this a pajama party." He sifted through my new clothes and pulled out a silk pajama set I had gotten free from my purchase at Victoria's Secret. The top was a black spaghetti strapped bralette with lace flirting across the cleavage and down to just above the navel; the matching shorts were silken with a hinting of lace across the bottom hem. I filed into the bathroom and changed into the ensemble, smiling at myself in the mirror before exiting back into my bedroom. Ravon threw a silver satin robe with black lace around the sleeves around my shoulders before leading me out of my bedroom.

"Where are we going? I thought we were going to watch the movie?" I asked, catching up to his quick pace, my naked feet padding against the dark hardwood flooring.

"Sweetie, we are, we're just going to watch it in the Theater Room." He shrugged, opening a door for me before corralling me inside. Rav flipped on the lights and worked with the projector while I took a seat in the middle of the six rows of theater seats. The seats themselves were obviously crazy comfortable, the cushions melding to my form and hugging my spine like I never new it needed. When the opening credits began, Ravon dimmed the lights and scrambled into the seat next to me. Fifteen minutes into the movie had me realizing that he was lying about the plot. Expecting a sweet movie about the obstacles of a young mute girl threw me through a hoop when the actual plot began to pan out.

"I don't like scary movies, you jerk!" I growled, pinching his bicep. Ravon grimaced and slapped my hand away, rubbing his wounded shoulder.

"I know that. How else would I get you to watch it?" He grumbled, turning back to the film. I crossed my arms over my chest, huffing irritably and wallowing in self pity. The door to the Theater Room opened, causing Ravon and I to squint painfully at the intruder.

"What are the two of you doing?" Nik questioned, walking down the aisle. I quickly looked away from him, allowing Ravon to indulge Nik on his scheme to give me nightmares for the next month. But out of the corner of my eye, I noticed he was both shirtless and wet, most likely having just showered.

"I'm forcing Ms. Sunshine to watch a horror film." Rav beamed, crossing his legs before drinking in the sight of Nik. "For what do we owe the pleasure?" Niklaus rolled his eyes, facing the projector's screen.

"Nothing, I was just checking in on her." He gave a curt wave. "I'll leave you to it." Ravon sprang up from his chair and grabbed Niklaus' hand, dragging him into the seat next to me.

"Don't be silly, Mr. Hale. This is no private showing, please, take a seat!" Rav insisted, sitting in the seat next to Niklaus, effectively caging him into the aisle. We all sat awkwardly for five minutes before Ravon pulled out his phone. "Oh my gosh, I'm so sorry to do this." I silently shook my head at him pleadingly.

Don't do this, I mouthed to him.

"This almost never happens; one of my clients is having a fashion emergency, but don't you two fret. I'm okay with you two finishing the movie without me." He got up from his seat and began walking toward the theater door. "Let me know if it's any good!"

"Haven't you seen this-" I began to say before Ravon had slipped out of the room. The air thickened considerably, the tension rising and rising. We hadn't spoken since that day he kissed me in the hallway and while I was used to Niklaus giving me the cold shoulder after intimate moments, I was dressed in a pair of highly revealing pj's, in a dark room with him in close proximity. I took a deep breath and focused on the screen in front of me, crossing my legs to avoid bumping him. My eyes followed the scared townspeople of Silent Hill file into a church while a large beast-like man with a triangular cage around his head chased after them. My fear grew as he took hold of a woman and I screamed as he ripped her clothes off. I couldn't watch anymore, but my eyes were glued to the screen. The beast-man ripped off the poor woman's skin and I lost it, throwing myself into Niklaus' lap and holding on for dear life. Nik hurriedly reached for the remote and paused the film, his hands gripping my hips and pulling me closer. One of his hands drifted to my back, rubbing soft soothing circular patterns into the satin robe, while his other hand came up to my cheek, pushing red hair away from my vision as I pressed my palms into my eyes.

"Shhh," He cooed softly, his thumb coming out to catch a tear that fell from my eye. "Have you never seen a horror movie before?" I silently shook my head, the image of the woman's skinless body burned into the flesh of my brain. He sighed softly and nodded, pulling my head into the nape of his neck before continuing to rub my back until my tears dried and my breathing went back to normal. The subtle smell of his cologne and aftershave mixed, and consumed me. The warmth of his bare chest radiated and comforted my previously distraught state. When I was fully calm, I slowly pulled away from his chest and looked down at my hands, embarrassed to have freaked out in front of him.

"I'm sorry," I bit my lip, avoiding his stare. "My father never allowed me to watch-"

"What are you wearing?" He asked suddenly, his eyes suddenly burning as they took in my choice of clothing. I paled, suddenly remembering the state I was in. Not only was I wearing the revealing pajamas, but I was also straddling a shirtless Niklaus.

Oh boy.

"This? Oh this." I pointed to the silk that covered little of my body. "Right, I got this when we went shopping last week."

"Oh no, no you didn't. I went in every store with you and I never saw you pick that shit out." He suddenly stopped, remembering the one store I had gone in alone. "Ah." I visibly swallowed and my cheeks burned. After a long moment, Nik's fingers came to the collar of my robe and slid down the fabric, feeling the satin on his skin. "Why did you get this?" My throat went dry and I struggled to come up with a reply. If I told him it was free, he would figure out I had bought something else in order to qualify for free items. But what was a believable lie?

"I-I like the way the silk felt," I mumbled softly, the temperature between our bodies becoming volcanic.

"Mm," He hummed approvingly, "So do I." His fingers drifted to my hips and he moved his hands to caress the silk that covered my thighs. "Oh, Baby Girl, what are you trying to do to me?" I took a deep breath, the fresh air in the room somehow had gotten sucked out and replaced with Florida-like humidity.

"Ravon picked it out for me." I whispered, my eyes becoming hooded as he massaged the curve of my hips. He growled quietly at my answer, his fingernails digging into my skin. "You realize he's gay, right?" I smiled softly, realizing how breathy my voice was beginning to sound.

"Doesn't matter." He grit, his tongue darting out to moisten his bottom lip. "Just because your father isn't here doesn't mean you need a man to boss you around." His words broke me from my heated trance and I pushed away from him, my ego having taken a blow.

"Fuck you, Nik." I scowled, walking as fast as I could and leaving the Theater Room. I didn't get far without Niklaus following from behind me.

"Two things, Princess: number one, did you just curse? And number two, what the fuck did you say to me?" He was hot on my trail, but I ignored him, rolling my eyes as he tried to get me to talk to him. When we got to my bedroom, I angrily poked at the keypad and slipped into the room before slamming the door shut. Feeling satisfied, I smirked at myself in the mirror. The door suddenly flung open again and I frowned. "You realize I have the code to your room as well, right?"

"Leave me alone, Nik." I warned, crossing my arms over my chest.

"Why? Since when do you make the orders?" He stalked toward me, his eyes scalding me into a statue where I stood. "You're just a daddy's girl and you know it. He says something and you do it. He tells you to wear something, you where it. He tells you to say something, you say it. Once a princess, always a princess."

"Hate to break it to you, Nik, but who are you to talk? You're here with me because your father told you to stick around and be my 'babysitter.'" I presented air quotes, remembering what he had said the first day we had met. Niklaus' jaw ticked and I knew I had hit a nerve. He spun on his heel and headed toward the door.

"Don't you fucking dare leave this room, Violet." He growled, reaching for the knob.

"Yes, Daddy." I spat and paled as he stopped mid-stride. It was a long moment before he turned his head to look at me, his eyes suddenly so dark, I thought they may have turned black.

"What did you just say?"

Chapter 13

"What did you just say?" He questioned, turning fully to face me. I let out a shaky breath, but held my ground, my fists balled fearfully under my arms that were still crossed over my chest.

"I said: yes, Daddy." My voice was strong, but I knew he could see through the facade. I was practically trembling and as if in one blink, he stood in front of me. His hard breathing fanning across my face as he himself struggled to stay in composure. One of his hands grasped my hip and shoved me toward the wall, my back laying flat against it as his fingers twisted into my hair and pulled my head forward, smashing my lips to his. I moaned into the kiss and Nik took his chance to deepen it, his tongue delving into my mouth and battled my own for dominance. When I quickly gave up, he massaged my tongue with his, his free hand slipping underneath the robe and pulling it off. The slight breeze caused me to shiver and Nik took this moment to pull away from me, pulling me toward the bed before he sat down and pulled me across his knees. With one hand still tangled in my hair, he used his other to graze over the silk that covered butt before delivering a hard smack to the cheeks.

"I want to hear you count each one out loud, Baby Girl." He growled before delivering another spank to my quickly reddening backside.

"Two," I whimpered, grimacing from the pain of the hit. He pressed, the palm of his hand coming out to sooth the ache of his previous blow, and I hoped he wouldn't venture further between my legs. It would be far more embarrassing for him to realize how much I enjoyed this. He delivered another smack and I cried out the adjoining number.

"Three!" My eyes squeezed shut and he soothed the pain with his palm once again. Another smack to my butt had me calling out four, then five, then six, and all the way up to ten. By the time Nik was finished with me, my backside burned without having to be touched. He marveled at the sight before he audibly gasped, his fingertips brushing the inside of my thighs.

"Fuck," He whispered beneath his breath, "Did you like when I spank you, Baby Girl?" I whimpered once more, wiggling to get of his hold before he pulled me upright, setting me in his lap to straddle his waist. His fingers trailed to just above my sex before he completely cupped it, my lungs gasping for air at the newfound sensation. "Well, it seems you did, you're soaked." He pulled back his hand to reveal his shining fingers, slick with my juices. I bit my lip hard, stuck between perpetual arousal and wavering embarrassment for having been wet from being spanked. Nik picked me up and threw me into the middle of my bed and with a mixture of fear, excitement, and anticipation, I trembled beneath him as he crawled over top of me, hovering above my burning skin. His lips pressed against mine once again, lavishing mine intimately before trailing kisses down my neck, sucking and nipping at my collarbones before coming to the silk of my top.

His brown eyes flickered up to mine, asking for approval to continue on and when I gave a slight nod, his fingertips grazed up my navel and beneath the lace of the bralette. When his fingers were securely latched around the fabric, he tore it away, the silk and lace ripping in half and discarded on the side of my bed. I squeaked in surprise and bit my lip shyly, watching him closely as he drank in the sight of my naked chest.

"God, so fucking perfect," He groaned, his fingers coming up the valley of my breasts before grazing over my right nipple, taking it between his fingertips before pinching it softly. I moaned at the twinge of pain that bled into a euphoric pleasure.

"Nik," I moaned out, his name falling from my lip involuntarily. His eyes shot to mine and he removed his hand from my breast, coming up and grabbing my chin between his thumb and index finger.

"Wrong, try again." He prompted, his opposite hand trailing circles around the areola of my left nipple. I searched my brain for the correct response, crying out from his incessant teasing.

"Niklaus," I tried, my eyelashes fluttering with anticipation. He shook his head against, dipping his head down to pepper the bulk of my breast with soft kisses, dodging my sensitive buds. I squirmed from beneath him and he smirked against me, moving to my opposite breast to torture it as well. I swallowed hard, biting my lip as his tongue dance around every part of my chest except the area I needed him most.

"Please," I was nearly sobbing, my core in a hailstorm of need. "Please, Daddy." I whispered and I felt his smirk deepen, his mouth finally enveloping that of my pink bud. I cried out in ecstasy, my hips bucking up against his, but one of his hands forced them down onto the bed. His tongue lavished my nipple before sucking its opposite into his mouth. I fisted the comforter that covered my bed, my eyes clenched with overwhelming rolls of pleasure that flowed to my sex. With his eyes trained on me, Nik began kissing down the length of my navel, his lack of warmth causing my chest to feel vulnerable and cold. His fingers played with the hem of my shorts and his eyes searched mine for consent.

"I've never done anything like-" He pressed his forefinger against my lips and gave a slight nod.

"I know, but I'm going to take care of you, Violet. You can trust me." He pressed a soft, sweet kiss against my lips before connecting our foreheads. "We can stop anytime you want."

"I trust you." I whispered softly and gave him the go-ahead to pull down my shorts. Nik's jaw fell open upon seeing me in full nude. His eyes became glued to the small, neat line of hair that lead to my sex. What can I say? The carpet matches the drapes.

"Fuck, Baby Girl, you're going to be the end of me." He growled, sinking onto his stomach and throwing my legs over his shoulders. I wasn't sure what to expect, I was completely new to this, but as he pressed his tongue flat against my sex, my back arched in greedy need.

"Oh my god," I cried out, my fingers tangling in his hair, drawing him impossibly closer. He smirked against me and held my thighs, his tongue rubbing figure-eights into my clit. Nik's tongue suddenly traveled south and slipped into my entrance, pulsing inside of me while one of his hand came out and rubbed at my sensitive bundle of nerves. I was seeing stars, my vision hazing as something within me built up. My legs began to shake, my toes curling in an overwhelming feeling. "Daddy, I'm- I-I'm-" And like a dam breaking, a wave of euphoria crashed through my entire being and I shook as I came down from the high, my breathing harsh and erratic. Nik reemerged from my sex, his lips glistening with the byproduct of my first orgasm. Climbing back over me, his fingers wrapped around my throat and he captured me in a hard kiss, his hands exploring my body now that his tongue had tasted it. Nik pressed his hips to mine and I gasped as his sweatpants-clad erection came in contact with my skin.

"Do you want to keep going?" He asked quietly between kissing down my neck. "We can stop, don't feel pressured-"

"Please, keep going." I placed my hands on his chest, our eyes connected as I felt down his chiseled abdomen before finding the waistband of his sweats and boxers. Lifting his hips, he helped me pull the fabric away and I gasped as the full length of his member pressed against my thigh. I would never want to further inflate Niklaus Hale's ego, but my god was he big. A surge of fear pierced through me and Nik kissed me ever so softly, caressing my cheekbone with his thumb.

"I'll go slow, okay, Baby Girl?" He said gently, pulling his wallet from the pocket of his sweat and retrieving a foil packet consisting of a condom. I gave a nod and prepared myself for the pain. Sliding the condom down his length, Nik positioned himself at my entrance, slowly rubbing it between my wet folds. I hummed in pleasure, enjoying the feeling of his skin against mine. But as he pressed against me, I stiffened, my heart hammering in my chest. "Baby, you've got to relax." Nik cooed, gathering my hair and wrapping it around his knuckles. I nodded softly for him to start and Nik's hips began to push forward, the head of his shaft burrowing inside my virgin canal. I cried out softly, burying my face in the crook of his neck. "Shhh, baby, the worst of it is over." After a moment of getting used to him, I pressed my hips forward for him to continue. Nik leaned down and kissed me softly, enveloping me in a heated kiss before thrusting the rest of himself inside of me. I screamed against his lips, the burning sensation causing a domino effect of pain to cascade through my body.

"Oh god, it hurts so bad." I dug my nails into his back and he groaned softly.

"Baby, you've got to stop otherwise I can't control myself." He said gently, but I could see his resolve diminishing. I took a deep breath and Nik sat up, pulling me into his lap to straddle him, his member still buried deep within me. "Move whenever you're ready, you're more in control this way." I nodded softly and after a few moments of adjustment, I began to move my hips to ride him. And oh, did the pain go away. In just a few minutes, I was rocking against his hips, my fingernails digging into his back and scratching down its entirety.

"Daddy," I cried out, my core pooling with the stirrings of another orgasm. Niklaus grabbed my waist and lifted me into the air, coming onto his knees and slammed into me relentlessly, his skin slapping against mine in hungry thrusts.

"So. Fucking. Tight." He grit out, his jaw ticking as the veins in his biceps bulged from holding me in the air. Suddenly, he pressed me into the bed, throwing one of my legs over my shoulder and driving into me like a man on a mission. His thumb coming out and busily stroking my clit to push me over the edge.

"Daddy, I'm going to come again." My back arched as Nik found a earth-shattering spot from within me.

"Right there, Baby Girl? Is that the spot?" He growled, his fingertips digging into my hips to pull me closer with each thrust. "Do you like my cock buried in that sweet pussy of yours?"

"Oh god, yes please!" I pleaded, my breasts bouncing with each of Nik's jutted movements. "Don't stop!" He pulled out of me and flipped me onto my stomach, entering me from behind. My mouth contorted into the form of an 'o,' the new position sending me through hoops.

"Come for me Violet, come around my dick." He moaned into my ear, his hand coming around us and rubbing sweet circles into my clit. As I was told, I came around Nik's shaft, his pulsing member being constricted by my tightness, pushing him into his own climax. "Fuck." Nik ground out, his jaw tick again as he emptied himself into the latex. With a deep sigh, I fell into the mattress, my eyes tiredly hooded and my body aching of exhaustion. Nik pulled the condom from his member and threw it into the waste bin before pulling out the covers from under me. Sliding in next to me, Nik pulled me into his chest and kissed the shell of my ear.

"That was amazing." I whispered as my eyes fell closed. "Is it always like that?"

"Is what always like that?" He whispered, his chin coming between my neck and my shoulder as he spooned me from behind.

"Sex," I mumbled, my mind falling further and further out of consciousness.

"No, Violet," He replied softly. "It's never been like that."

Chapter 14

Niklaus

My eyes peeled open, the soft light from the night-stand allowing some sort of soft, yellow tinted visibility. My head felt warm against the flesh it was resting against and I hummed at the thought of the woman I was laying upon, my arms wrapped securely around her small waist. I lifted my chin to look at her and couldn't help but smirk at the sight. My head had been resting between her milky tits, the soft pink nipples pebbled as the cool air hardened them by the absence of the blanket I had over top of me. Violet's chest slowly moved up and down, her beautiful lips slightly parted in her slumbered state.

Fuck, she is gorgeous.

I took a moment to fully take her in, to appreciate the markings I had left on her no longer virgin body. The periwinkle colored bruises that littered her hips, the love bites across her collarbones and bust, the swell of her sweet lips. With a pleased sigh, I slowly pulled my arms from around her and lifted the blanket to her chin. Slipping into my joggers,

I glanced at the clock and realized it was already eight the next morning. Fucking into exhaustion does that to a person, I guess.

I quietly left Violet's room and made my way to my own, yearning for a warm shower and a change of clothing. Once in the solitude of my own room, I slid out of the joggers and hopped into the shower. The water beat against my aching muscles, despite having slept on a five thousand dollar mattress that the King of New York had footed the bill for. Oh shit.

Talon Maddox.

Oh shit, oh fuck, oh shit!

I paced the length of my shower, my hand rubbing my chin as I finally thought through what I had done. I fucked the Princess of Manhattan; and god did I want to do it again, and again, and again. My mind shifted the the redhead I had dug my own grave over, the image of her hair splayed across the pillows as I thrust into her, her lips pouted in begging. Daddy, Daddy, Daddy...

I shook her out of my head. Focus. No one can find out about this; if her father didn't kill me, her brothers would. I know the Maddox boys, and I know their father. Violet's smile suddenly popped into my head, her cheeks bright and flushed, her straight white teeth grinning at me. My muscles relaxed and I began to think about her laugh, the way her small had fit in my big one, the fact that only the redhead calls me Nik.

A deep sigh left my lips and I shut off the water. Drying off with a plush black towel, I slid it across my hips and tied it off. Quickly finding a dark navy blue v-neck t-shirt and a pair of black jeans, I pulled on the ensemble and stuffed my feet into a pair of black Adidas Superstars. Making my way to the kitchen, I began to order around the staff, making sure this morning's breakfast would not only be delicious, but would take a little while to prepare. Sitting in my chair at the dining room table, I began to file through payroll, as was my job before Violet had come along. A pair of feet padded into the room and I smirked down at the table, scribbling my signature on a check before sitting back in the chair and drinking in the sight of her, like a man deprived of sustenance.

Violet

Niklaus' stared began at my feet, traveling up my bare legs and up by silken robe-clad body. I bit my lip bashfully, looking down at my toes and suddenly unable to meet his heated gaze. A deep chuckle filled the air and my cheeks flushed.

"Good morning, Kiska [Kitten]." He spoke lowly, his tongue wrapping around the last word like it were a lollipop.

"Morning," I replied, my voice high and embarrassingly squeaky.

"Come here." He ordered, his voice firm, but soft around the edges. With my feet still on the dark hardwood floor, I padded my way over to where he was sitting. Once we were nearly a foot away from each other, I stopped, my head feeling fuzzy in his presence. His large hands reached out and gripped my hips, pulling me between his knees before lifting me onto the table. My teeth bit into my bottom lip further, his eyes looking up at me in an attempt to meet my own. "How did you sleep?"

"Like a log," I snorted before realizing what I had said. Was that my best attempt at sexy? I could've said something smooth, something better than a reference to a piece of wood. I mentally face-palmed as his lips quirked into a cheesy smile. "What's for breakfast." His smile slid into a smirk and my stomach erupted into butterflies.

"Well, I'm glad you said something because I'm absolute-ly starved." His hand pressed against my navel and gently pushed my back against the table, laying me flat while he spread my legs to his viewing.

"Oh my god, Nik-" I squealed, pinching my legs together while looking both ways in embarrassment.

"Don't worry, Kiska, the kitchen staff is busy making your breakfast and my second meal of the day." He peeled my legs apart, his breath fanning against my sex. "You're all mine." His tongue was suddenly against my clit and I cried out in un-foreseen pleasure, my toes curling with the euphoric feeling. My breathing became shallow and fast, my heart hammering in my chest as I thought about the idea of someone walking in at any given moment with Niklaus' head buried between my legs. The thought scorched my core and my fingers found his hair, tugging him closer for needed friction. I was beyond sore from last night's activities, but this made up for it.

Nik's lips circled around my sensitive bud and sucked before his tongue dipped into my womanhood, quickly pulsing in and out of me. My back arched against the table, my knuckles growing white as I fisted his black curly locks. My hips began to buck, but Nik's hands held me down, leaving me at his mercy.

"Daddy," I called out softly, moaning around the name. His grip tightened and he slid me closer, the papers beneath me allowing me to slide effortlessly toward Nik's hungry mouth. His right had fell from my hip and he pressed two fingers against my lips. Opening my mouth, I sucked digits like a pornstar, bobbing my head and swirling my tongue around them before he moaned out my name and pulled them from my lips. His mouth was suddenly void and I whimpered, my inner walls clenching with need.

"Who makes you feel good, babygirl?" Niklaus hummed, his two fingers suddenly sliding through my slick sex.

"You do," I groaned, my hips bucking once more with clear need. Nik's opposite hand parted the top of my robe, exposing my breasts to the room. Taking one hardened bud between his finger, Nik pulled and twisted it with slight roughness, but the dull pain ignited a fire in me, my hips surging forward and sinking down onto his fingers.

"Fuck," He moaned, his voice like gravel as he watched me fuck myself on his fingers. My core began to build and build, and build until I was so close to falling over the edge, I could taste it. "So fucking beautiful, Violet." Nik growled as he watched me come undone, shaking as the orgasm racked through my body. As I finished, Nik removed his fingers and drank up my excess. My body became jelly-like and noticing this, he pulled my robe over my exposed body and pulled me into his lap. The kitchen bell rang and the staff filed into the room, placing plates of food across the table.

"Thank you," Nik nodded and they left the room, his hand coming out to move the red blanket of hair I had covered my flushed face with. "Nothing is more beautiful than this." His index finger and thumb gripped my chin and he brought his lips to mine. I lost myself in the slow kiss, his lips bringing me to oblivion as I savored this, savored him. As he pulled away, he pressed a soft kiss to my forehead and turned me toward the table, one hand wrapped around my waist to secure my place on his lap.

"Now eat, Kiska," He mused as he placed a plate in front of me. "Unlike myself, you have not quenched your hunger."

Chapter 15

Violet

"Lottie, please," Ravon begged, his hands positioned as though he were praying. I delicately painted silvery iron bars onto the canvas. It had taken me two days to get this far, but I was almost finished. The forest green ivy that crawled up the wall contrasted beautifully the dark red brick. I took a step back to admire my work, my heart warming at the portrait of my family home back in New York, painted from memory. "Darling, please focus, I'm in a dire situation that you, and you alone, can help me with." Sighing softly, I turned to face my best friend.

"Tell me what I'd have to do again?" I pulled off my art smock and slid past Ray, making my way to the bathroom to wash up.

"Double date with me at The Vortex tonight," Ravon recited exasperatedly, following me into the bathroom as I undressed from my sweats and plain t-shirt. Pulling the glass door open, I hopped into the shower and allowed the hot beads of water to bounce off of my skin. "It's Halloween babe, so all you need to do is wear the cute little costume I made for you and if your love for me doesn't make you want to do me this favor... Then I'll buy drinks for you all night."

"I'm not interested in drinking," I called over the noise of the shower.

"Fine, don't drink. Dance, hang out with Klaus outside of this damn house for once, c'mon, please!" Ravon whined from behind the glass. I bit my lip softly and finished up my shower, lathering my hair in coconut hair gel before and conditioner before washing everything out, and exiting the shower. Ravon wrapped a towel around me tightly and I beamed at him in thanks.

"Nik is going?" I tried to remain as though I was unfazed by this new information, but it bothered me that he had never mentioned it. We'd spent nearly every moment together in the last forty-eight hours, perhaps he hadn't wanted me to know, it's not like we are an official couple. Ravon's eyes glinted mischievously.

"His name was on the list for tonight," He bit his lip to suppress an excited smile, "I'll be back at seven to help you get ready, see you later babe!" Ray kissed my cheek before leaving my bedroom. I sprawled out on my bed, opening up "Love Warrior" and diving into its literary goodness. Forty-five minutes into reading, the door to my bedroom reopened, showing a coy Niklaus in its feat.

"Hey," I called, shutting the book quietly and sitting up straighter.

"Malishka," He greeted delicately, shutting the door softly behind himself and crawling onto the bed. Laying his head in my lap, I began to absentmindedly play with his curls. An annoying urge to ask about the club began to bubble in my stomach, my jaw clenching slightly to refrain my lips from uttering my insecurities. Niklaus is not my boyfriend, I have no business to be meddling in his affairs beyond Hale Manor. "You're quiet," He observed, "What's wrong?"

"Nothing," I tried come off as indifferent, but my voice came out squeaky and high-pitched.

"Malishka [Baby]," He warned lowly, his head picking up to look at me through his locks.

"It's seriously nothing; Ravon asked me to go out with him and his new boyfriend tonight," I bit my lip, feeling my cheeks heat up at how ridiculous I sounded, "He said you were already planning on going…So maybe we could double date." Nik's mouth formed a thin line as he took in what I said, his brow furrowing in on his eyes.

"I actually wasn't going to go, my name is always on that list as the Hale's own The Vortex," He took my chin between his thumb and index finger. "I thought we'd pig-out on some Halloween candy and watch a couple Halloween movies tonight, but if you want to go to the club, that is also doable."

After an hour of getting ready, Ravon and I stepped out of my bedroom. Ray had put together a little devil costume for me, consisting of a short red dress, a pair of matching strappy heels, and a pair of red devil horns attached to a headband. He had spent the past hour putting my hair up into a loose bun, allowing a few tendrils of curled hair to escape past my hairline and temples. Collecting my things into my sparkly red handbag, I followed Ravon into the main foyer where Niklaus waited for us. Ravon had put together an angel costume for Nik to wear; a pair of white straight legged slacks with a white button-down dress shirt that Nik had shoved the long sleeves up to his biceps, coupled with a pair of white lace-up Oxford shoes and a silver halo atop his head. Upon hearing our footsteps nearing, Nik turned to face us, his mouth going slack at the sight of me.

"No, absolutely not, we're trying not to draw attention to her, Ravon." He pointed to the dress, pulling the fabric back before letting it snap back against my body, "This is practically strapping neon signs to her that say 'Hey, look at me!'" Ravon rolled his eyes, readjusting the leaves that were sewn onto his nude briefs.

"Oh, please, you're just worried other guys are going to be looking at her fine self, live in the twenty-first century with us, Klaus! Women wear what they want!" Ravon snapped his fingers at Nik and grabbed my hand, pulling me out of the door and into the Hale's black BMW. Niklaus followed behind us gruffly, his lips almost set into a pout. The car ride was filled with Ravon gushing over his new boyfriend, Jeremiah, whom he had met at a catwalk show in the city. When we arrived, Niklaus was quick to grab my hand, securing me to his side as we walked past the long line of people waiting outside The Vortex. Music blared from the speakers, a live DJ stood at the far end of the room shuffling through albums as people danced just a few feet below him. Ravon gave a squeal of excitement as he sprang into the arms of a large man, his muscles reflecting the strobe lights as the florescence dance around the room. The man, who I assumed to be Jeremiah, was matching Ravon in his nude briefs which had leaves sewn into the fabric.

"What are they meant to be dressed up as?" Nik questioned, his voice just loud enough to be heard over the heavy music.

"Ravon said they're supposed to be Adam and Steve." I emphasized the last name and Nik's eye shot up in recognition, a smile sprouting on his lips.

"Always so clever," He chuckled softly and Ravon nodded in thanks, a bright smile on his face as he embraced his boyfriend.

"Attention everyone, the pole dancing competition will be starting in thirty minutes," The DJ stated over the heavy base of the current song that was playing. My eyes drifted to the five poles that were lined up near the DJ's setup and a twist of excitement riddled my belly.

"That sounds like fun," I yelled to Ravon who nodded enthusiastically.

"I'm going to get everyone drinks. Nik, Lottie, what do you want?" Ravon took our orders to the bar and came back with a tray. I sipped at my Pepsi, feeling odd being the only one not drinking alcohol. Nik tossed back the glass of scotch that he had ordered while Ravon nursed his Sex on the Beach. Nik and Jeremiah fell into conversation related to book work, which lead me to find out Jeremiah was an accountant.

"Excuse us," Ravon flashed a quick smile to our dates before grabbing my hand and pulling me into the crowd. "I thought we'd get a little dance in before our boys swooped us away from each other, I need at least one dance with my girl." Ravon winked, leading me into the sea of people grinding against each other. I grinned in excitement, my heart brightening at my best friend's gesture. Looking back to Niklaus, my eyes took in the curly haired man who had suddenly taken up conversation with a sexy nurse at the bar, her hand coming out to his arm and slowly moving down until their fingers met. Jealousy began to boil my blood, my face becoming unbearable hot. "Ray, what if we did that instead?" I nodded toward the stage and Ravon clapped his hands excitedly.

Niklaus

"Where are they?" I asked Jeremiah as I glanced down at my watch. It had been almost fifteen minutes and the devil and her counterpart hadn't returned to our table. Jeremiah gave a brief shrug, taking a swig of his beer before setting it back on its coaster. "I'll be back." I disappeared into the crowd before hearing Jeremiah's reply. Weaving through the mass of people took even longer than I had expected. My eyes scanned the room as I neared the stage, my heart began to race in my chest.

Where the fuck is she?

Five spotlights suddenly popped onto the stage, each shining on a woman standing in front of a exotic dancing pole. The first two girls were unrecognizable, however the third girl in the lineup was the nurse who had approached me at the bar. It took me a few minutes to get her to back off, but I could see she wasn't through with me yet. She sent me a wink from the stage and I grimaced and moved my eyes to the next dancer. I couldn't help but grin at the Steve who was spinning around the pole like an expert on stage. Jeremiah whistled appreciatively from the bar and Ravon visibly blushed. But if Ravon is up there, than...

My eyes fell upon the little devil the the little red dress. Her legs were crossed innocently as she nervously looked out over the crowd. A territorial snarl ripped from my lips as I heard several men in the crowd comment on her body and what they would like to do to it. I was about to hop on stage and pull her off when the DJ pulled out his microphone and started the competition. He interviewed each contestant and allowed them to explain what their costume was, and why they chose it.

"And who do we have here? We have a little she-devil in our midst, my friends." The DJ chuckled circling around Violet like a predator watching over its prey. "What's your name, beautiful?" He held out the microphone to Violet who paled at the question.

"Um," She swallowed, "Nicole." Her eyes met mine and I couldn't help but smirk at the fake name.

"Well, Nicole, why have you picked to be a devil, this Samhain evening?" The DJ questioned, putting the mic back to Violet's lips.

"This costume was actually made for me by my best friend," She glanced at Ravon with adoration before meeting my eyes once again. "But I've also been known to be a little naughty from time to time." My cock went rigid, my sudden erection straining against my slacks uncontrollably.

"I believe that." The DJ laughed softly. "Well, I wish you luck in tonight's competition. Now since you're known to be a little naughty, how about you pick the song." Violet followed him up to his setup where they flipped through a variety of songs. When she returned to her pole, she faced toward the crowd, her innocent stance replaced with one of confidence. The song started and I felt my pulse quicken, my eyes glued to the woman I was going to severely punish at the end of the night.

Her hips bent forward and her upper torso went with it, her arms stretching to the extent over the glowing legs, her slender fingers traveling up the milky skin slowly in tune with the song. Once upright again, she hooked her leg around the pole, supporting her body weight with one hand around the metal, and slowly leaned back, her red hair spilling from the confines of the bun she once had had it tied up in. The crowd cheered, all eyes on the beautiful fire-haired woman on the last pole despite the other dancers trying their best.

I can do it slow now, tell me what you want

The song continued and Violet followed, both of her hands now on the pole as she picked up speed and twisted around, her feet leaving the floor as she held herself up, spinning around the circumference. Catching herself near the bottom, Violet slowly stood back up, her clothed genitalia grazing the pole seductively. Swinging back around the pole, one leg hooked under herself as the other protruded out at a ninety degree angle, her head thrown back in faked ecstasy. When her ass met with the floor, she laid her back against the floor of the stage and lifted her legs, rolling over onto her knees with her backside now in the air. My erection was painful and I yearned to fuck that little she-devil right against that pole. But despite my need, I continued to watch, mesmerized by her effortless movements.

Slowly climbing back to her feet, she bent over and held onto the bottom of the pole before wiggling her hips, causing her ass cheeks to jiggle in ripples from beneath her dress. Tossing her head back, her hair fell sexily around her shoulders as she slowly stalked around the pole, her eyes never leaving mine. One of her arms came up as far as she could reach on the pole, the other coming down to attach to the lowest part of the pole that she could grab before her feet lifted and she swung around the pole once again. Her knees gently hit the floor and she followed the music back to her feet.

We can go another round if that's what you want

Grabbing the pole and spreading her legs shoulder-width apart, she swung her hips slowly toward the pole and her upper body followed slowly behind, the sheer sight of her grinding against the pole sending my nerves into overdrive. Swinging her hips back and forth, slowly pulled away from the pole and grabbed a chair that was near the back of the stage. Once the chair was sat in the view of the audience, she approached the edge of the stage and pointed to me. I shook my head, my raging erection not allowing me to move.

"I'll go up there-" A guy from behind me purred and I growled, hoisting myself onto the stage and awkwardly making my way over to the chair. Shoving me into the seat, Violet stalked around me, her index finger grazing across my chest and shoulders until she stood in front of me. Turning to the crowd, she bent until she was nearly sitting in my lap before rolling her hips. My hands couldn't help but come out to feel her generous ass, staking claim to what was mine and only mine. Turning around to face me, she crouched down and slapped her hand between my legs, her palm hitting the metal of the chair. Standing straight again, she placed her high heeled foot in the space between my legs and placed my hand on her thigh before her hips rolled once again, her pussy so close to my face my mouth began to water. Pulling away suddenly, she turned back toward the crowd and pulled my hands to her hips, slowly grinding down until her ass met with my crotch.

I decided this was enough and I stood, grabbing her hand before pulling her off the stage. The DJ laughed into the microphone and pronounced Nicole the winner before I pulled her into the street. Hailing my driver, the black BMW pulled up and I helped Violet inside.

"What about Ravon and Jere-" She began, her face flush from the active workout she had just committed.

"I'll send the car back," I leaned into her ear, my teeth grazing her lobe with promise of her ruin. "You're in so much fucking trouble."

Chapter 16

V iolet

My eyes reluctantly peeled opened, meeting the sight of immaculate black Victorian designs crawling across the ceiling surrounding a beautiful black chandelier. My jaw fell down to my throat as I yawned tightly, my head shifting to the side before gathering a mouthful of dark brown curls. Choking slightly, I scooted away from the hard wall of muscle I had been sleeping against and reached above my head to stretch my arms, my tiptoes curling at the satisfying extension of body. Grimacing slightly, I whimpered quietly in pain as I sat up to assess myself. Slipping from the lush black silk covers of Niklaus' bed, I tiptoed to the bathroom and flicked on the light switch. My nudity was littered with love bites and bruises, my hips held purple and blue fingerprints, my ass still pink from the outrageous amount of spankings I had received, the space around my areolas bitten and sucked until they turned periwinkle in color. My core clenched at the remembrance of his touch, rough and than soothing, harsh and than soft. A pair of large hands wrapped around my small wrists, his lips coming down to kiss the yellowing bruises that had been left behind.

"Was I a tad too rough, Malishka?" His rough morning voice lulled in my ear as he came back up from my wrists. I shook my head, stepping back into his warmth as he pulled me into his chest.

"Nothing I couldn't handle," He spun me around on my heel, lifting my bare butt onto the marble sink and capturing my lips in a soft, lingering kiss.

"Mm," He hummed in approval, tracing the curve of my spine with his fingertips. "Punishment looks good on you."

Niklaus helped me from the vehicle, but before my heels could even meet the ground, I was thrown over his shoulder. My heart raced with excitement. His chest had risen and fallen so quickly while we rode back to Hale Manor, so angry and lustful that he shook.

"Nik!" I cried out as he carried me into the large home, slamming the door behind himself. He didn't flatter me with a response, but instead took me deeper into the household. "You passed my bedroom." He, again, gave me no response but kicked open a room I had never been in before. Pulling me into the darkness, Nik threw me onto a plush service and moved around the room with ease despite there being no visible light. A drawer opened and shut, footsteps neared me and my right wrist was captured in a satin-like fabric that was restrained against a wooden post. My left wrist followed suit and was tightly secured to a separate post.

"Nik...?" I called questioningly into the dark, tense air. A lamp was switched on and he bore down at me with intent, his eyes falling across my skin and turning it to fire. I squirmed with desire, his mouth tightened as he appraised my condition; tied up to a bed's headboard, my breasts almost falling out from the top of my dress, my thighs clenched with pooling need.

"Where did you learn to dance like that, Violet?" He spoke softly, but with conviction.

"Dance class, ballet..." I swallowed thickly as he made his way around the bed, hunger in his dark eyes, "Haven't you ever seen Flashdance?" He was quiet for a moment reaching forward, his fingers tracing the outline of my jawline, moving lower down my throat until he met the valley of my breasts.

"Ravon will be so upset," Nik sighed softly, feigning disappointment. Before I could question him, Niklaus' fingers tore the fabric down the middle, exposing my naked chest to the sauna-like bedroom. My nipples pebbled beneath his stare, without even having been touched. The mere sensuality of the moment caused my core to tighten and my hips rocked upward in response. Niklaus growled lowly in his throat, taking in the sight of my heavy, deprived breasts and white lacy thong-clad lower region. My body was beginning to ache from the lack of touch and with my restraints, I was forced to writhe under Nik's gaze. "You know how fucking pissed I am at you?" His fingers found my left nipple, pinching it before my back arched with unmeasured pleasure.

"No," I squeaked, Nik's mouth wrapped around my nipple and soothed the dull pain that his fingers had left behind. He pulled away just enough for his mouth to hover over the bud.

"Every guy in a mile radius was looking at you grind on that pole, babygirl. Meanwhile, I'm stuck out in the audience with a ragingly hard cock." He sighed deeply, his teeth grazing my sensitive nipple once again before moving to it's twin. moved an inch up from my bud and sunk his teeth into my skin, his tongue lavishing the area with a soothing pattern. Several bites later, Nike moved down my navel, his hands openly fondling my thighs and rubbing them up and down but never touching the area I needed him most. Throwing my legs apart, a cold breeze was blown against my wetness. Niklaus' index finger pulled the lace aside to view my womanhood, another growl surfacing from his throat at its sight. The bed shifted as he crawled onto the king-sized mattress, moving toward me on his hands and knees.

"Please, Daddy!" I cried, my ankles hooking under the back of his knees to pull him closer. Delivering a light slap to my mound, Niklaus roughly grabbed my hip and forced it into submission. "Please."

"I decide when you feel good, babygirl, understand?" He hovered over my body for a moment before kissing me roughly, his tongue devouring my mouth like a man deprived of sustenance. When my lips were red and swollen, Nik pulled away and positioned himself back at my core. Without warning, two of his digits entered me, causing my eyes to roll into the back of my head.

"You're so fucking wet it's ridiculous, fuck Violet." He groaned, pumping his fingers faster and faster, curling them to the soft spot that made me see stars. I cried out, begging for more, tears gathering in my eyes as I plead for release. Ignoring my pleas, Niklaus continued his torture, bringing me close to climax before slowing his pace and allowing me to come back down before building me back up. My skin developed a sheen of glowing sweat, my toes sore from having been curled so hard for so long. "You want my cock, babygirl?" He spat, thumbing my clit with ever syllable he spoke.

"Please, please fuck me, Daddy." I moaned out in tired need. Nik suddenly flipped me onto my knees, the restraints causing my wrists to cross painfully in front of me, but that that was far from my conscious mind. Positioning myself at his will, my ass stood proudly in the air waiting for attention. His warm hands smoothed over the skin on my bottom, appreciating its expanse before slapping my left cheek. He hummed as it jiggled and I whimpered from beneath him.

"You know what to do," He said softly, soothing the pink hand print he had left on my butt cheek .

"One," I counted aloud, grimacing once again as spanked me once again. "Two."

"You want my cock?" The sound of clothes falling on the floor made my stomach flip with anticipation. Yes, this is what I wanted. He wrapped my hair around his hand and pulled my head back, forcing me to look at him. "Fuck yourself." My core burned with his racy comment and gasped as the tip of his dick ran between my slick folds. Needing no further instruction, I slowly sunk down onto his length. With a deep growl, Nik delivered another spanking to my ass. "Keep going."

"Three," I moaned, the spankings adding a painful hum to my uncontrollable pleasure. My hips bounced with vigor, finding a pleasing pace as I rocked against Niklaus' thick thighs. He snarled wildly, loving the image of me fucking myself on his manhood. By spanking number thirty-four, Nik could no longer handle my pace and seized my hips roughly, his fingernails biting into my skin before thrusting into me completely, his balls flush against my bottom. I cried out in surprise, my mouth in a permanent 'o' shape as he feverishly plowed into my sex. Allowing one of his hands to drop from my waist, Nik heatedly rubbed my clit, causing my vision to blur.

"I'm going to- I'm going to-" My eyes clenched shut as Nik gave one last laborious thrust into me, setting off our simultaneous climax.

"You've been quiet, is everything okay?" Nik said quietly, having made a bath for us that consisted of lavender bath salts and lemongrass essential oil. Bubbles covered my private parts as I leaned against his nakedness from beneath the water. Had I not already been wet, Nik would've noticed my arousal. Pushing back all of my erotic thoughts, I turned over in the tub and hugged his torso, resting my chin on his chest.

"I am wonderful." I smiled softly, the bath salts and essential oil relaxing my muscles into a pudding-like state. Running his fingers through my untangled locks, he pressed a gentle kiss to my forehead. We stayed in the bath for twenty more minutes before Nik helped me out of the tub and we dried off. Walking back to my bedroom, Nik promised me a pancake breakfast in bed, to which I giddily agreed. I jumped into my bed excitedly, tearing the damp towel from my body and snuggling under the cool covers. I pulled a book I hadn't yet finished from my nightstand and delved into the material. After a little under fifteen minutes of waiting, the pressurized door to my room opened with an audible hiss. My heart thumped erratically in my chest at the thought of the curly-haired man who was bringing me pancakes. Sitting up with just a blanket to cover my chest, I grinned at the opening door.

"Well that didn't take you too long, Dad-"

My heart dropped.

My face paled.

Our eyes met.

I gasped.

He dropped the bag of McDonald's food.

"Valen," I whispered. "What are you doing here?" My twin's eyes took in the sight of my barely covered nude state, piecing the image together with my previous statement, his face mirrored my own. We stood frozen for several minutes, neither of us knowing what to say or do. My bedroom door opened once again with a smiling Niklaus Hale, two plates full of decadent fluffy pancakes, butter, and syrup.

"Just as promised, a pancake breakfast for my babygirl." His smile suddenly faltered, realizing we had company. But not just any company, the company of my brother. "Fuck."

Chapter 17

N iklaus

Valen made it known that he would be extending his stay while covering for my relationship with his twin. Putting him up in the west wing, Violet and I allowed him to settle in and unpack his belongings. Violet was nearly bursting with excitement and while I was happy for her happiness, I couldn't help but feel disappointed that all of her attention was no longer on me, which only brought me to question of: What are we? I separated from the little minx and changed into some workout clothes from my bedroom, needing some time on my own to think. Once I got to the in-home gym, I plugged the aux cord into my cell and used a playlist off of YouTube, pulling my hair in a bun at the crown of my scalp. After an hour on the treadmill, I shifted to cleans and shoved a hundred pound weight on each side before beginning. The song shifted to a faster pace beat and I went along with the music, swinging the bar up and under my chin before letting it fall to the ground; repeat. After twenty of these, I pulled the weights off and started toward the dumbbells. Pulling the fifties out, I worked my left arm and then the right, alternating between the two. I closed my eyes to focus on the pain of my muscles being worked, the music pulsing into my eardrums.

A small pair of hands wrapped around my chest and I dropped the bells, the feeling of her fingertips drifting up my abdomen made my mind clear. I didn't care what we were, I just wanted her all to myself; mind, body, soul. All of it. I wanted her marked with my name and I wanted to bare hers. A connection like this was nothing I ever imagined, she was a poison and an antidote all in one. I would risk anything for this girl and it scared the hell out of me. Opening my eyes, I watched her hands slide up my shoulder and slowly work at the tense muscles, earning a low groan from my lips. Her hands were suddenly missing from my body and my body went cold without her warm touch. Turning in her direction, she was already walking toward the leg press. Adding almost two-hundred and fifty pounds to the machine, she sat at an angle and began pumping her thighs from a crouched stance to completely straight legs.

"Christ Malishka, I knew you had great legs but I had no idea you worked out." I ogled at her, biting my tongue as my eyes drifted across her tight ass.

"Yeah, well, I've slacked the past two months. I had no idea there was a gym here until one of the maids told me you had gone to work out." She did ten more reps and then used a lever to halt the weights. Once she was standing once again,

I collected her in my arms and kissed down her neck. She hummed softly as my tongue drifted down her collarbones, but she pushed gently against my chest and I placed her back on her feet. "I actually did come in here to work out, Mr. Hale." She giggled and drifted over to the punching bags, wrapping her hands before lowering into the proper stance and attacking the bag. My eyebrows shot up in surprise and while it made sense she knew how to box because of her lineage, it surprised me that Talon Maddox had even allowed his precious daughter to participate in such a sport.

"Want to spar?" She cocked an eyebrow at me. "You keep staring, so I'm assuming you want a chance at all this." She motioned to her biceps and I rolled my eyes, a smirk coming across my mouth.

"You can't handle me, babe." I nodded toward the ropes of the boxing ring to her right, which we usually used for training purposes when we added new guys to our crew, but I wouldn't mind throwing Violet around a little. "But I can take it easy on you."

"If you say so," She smirked as if she knew something I didn't. Climbing through the ropes, I leaned against one corner of the ring and she bounced from one leg to the other opposite of me.

"No face or genitalia hits, I think that's a given." I said, stating my conditions to this little match. She gave a curt nod and bumped her fists together, ready to start in on me. My smirk growing deeper, I slowly stepped forward. My thought process was to allow her the first hit and then from there, I would gently, but firmly show her who's boss. She bobbed forward and faked a left hook, squaring me on the right shoulder. Wincing with painful surprise, I stumbled backward and gaped at her. She innocently shrugged and I quickly charge forward, only for her to duck beneath me and knee me in the ass. "Fuck, Violet!" Merely giggling, she zig-zagged around me and climbed on my back from behind, hooking her legs around my knees and jerking sideways, causing me to fall on my sore ass. She stood over me, her legs on either side of my stomach as she watched me from above, pleased with herself.

"How?" I groaned, wincing at the painful ache in my back.

"Fifteen years of Jujutsu and five years of boxing," She smiled proudly and I rolled my eyes, grabbing her ankle and pulling it out from under her. When she fell to her knees, I flipped us over and held her arms above her head. She struggled for a moment, only to realize I was not fascinated by labored breathing that was causing her chest to very nearly fall from the top of her shirt. Pressing my erection against her thigh, she moaned and her irises darkened, pressing her hips up to meet mine.

After we finished up in the gym and cleaned up our mess, I pulled Violet into my bedroom to share a shower with me. Having had her sweet little pussy wrapped around my cock as she rode me into oblivion on the boxing ring floor had milked me of whatever seed I had left for the day. But washing her beautiful curves gave me immense pleasure beyond bodily satisfaction. I lathered my hands full of soap and touched every part of her body and while it was not sexual, it was incredibly intimate. Our eyes never leaving each other, our breathing in sync and causing the glass around my shower to fog even more so than the heat of the shower. Once she was completely clean and I gave myself a good wash, we stepped out of the shower onto the blush memory foam rug just outside of the tub before I wrapped a towel around her small frame. We spent the rest of the day naked under my comforter, our limbs tangled together while we watched Christmas specials on Netflix. So much time had passed that we had missed lunch, which was odd for someone with as big of an appetite as Violet. A knock sounded at my door and I hollered to whoever it was to leave.

"I'm terrible sorry Mr. Hale, however, your guest Mr. Maddox is asking to have dinner with you and Ms. Maddox." Violet and I exchanged looks and I pulled out my cell to glance at the time. Sure enough, it was almost seven o'clock in the evening and we had barely left my bedroom. Violet snuck off to her bedroom to make herself look decent and I threw on a plain white tee and a pair of black joggers before making my way to the dining hall. Violet arrived ten minutes later with her brother at her side, their arms linked and despite the obvious relation, the intimate touch made my blood boil. Violet sat across from me and her brother took the seat at her side. Just as one of the kitchen aides were about to take my order, Ravon flitted into the room, pulling the chair beside me from the table and taking a seat.

"This must be Violet's twinny I've been hearing so much about," Ray shook the redhead's hand from across the table. "Gosh, your parents must be gorgeous, I mean look at the two of you! Y'all could be models." Violet playfully rolled her eyes and Valen laughed softly. "I'm your sister's self-appointed best friend, Ravon Yorkshire, a pleasure to meet you."

"Name's Valen, but you can call me Val." The redhead chuckled. We ordered our food and the three fell into a comfortable conversation, while I became lost within my own thoughts.

"What's the plan, Klaus?" Valen questioned from across the table. I blinked a few times before truly focusing at the three pairs of eyes looking at me. Our food arrived and I leaned back in my chair.

"Sorry, what was that?" I questioned, thanking the waitstaff as they exited the room.

"What's your plan for when your father comes back to Chicago? Are you going to tell him about you and Lottie, or are you guys breaking it off? I'm only asking because I want to cover my own tracks as best as possible. I'd like it if we were all on the same page, as all of the people who know about the two of you is in this room, correct." Valen quirked an eyebrow at me and I shrugged.

"Everyone but Sebastian-"

"Sebastian knows about us?" Violet inquired, placing a forkful of pot roast into her mouth. I the fork leave her lips and I lost my train of thought, fuck Niklaus, get it together.

"Yes, he made a guess and I it was hard to deny." I replied to which she gave a soft nod.

"Who is Sebastian?" Valen asked, looking between me and his sister.

"My best friend, we can trust him." I said as I cut into my own plate of pot roast. Valen crossed his arms across his chest, his lips pursed into a thin line.

"Alrighty then, so we are back to my original question: what is your plan?" He stared at me blankly, as if he knew I didn't have one. My skin suddenly felt heated and I forced away the urge to strangle the man to shut him up.

"Well, I haven't yet figured one out. Violet and I haven't really talked about it." I said popping a soft carrot into my mouth.

"You must at least know if you want to continue or not? I mean, from there it should be easy." As Valen spoke, I noticed Violet's eyes drift to her lap and I could feel how uncomfortable she was getting, and while I knew she wanted the answers to this question herself, I couldn't bear to continue this conversation with an audience.

"With all due respect to you and your family, I don't think it's any of your business as of right now. If Violet and I haven't spoken to each other about it, I should hardly be the one in charge of making decisions on her behalf." I continued eating without another word, not because I was angry with Valen for putting me on the spot, but because I was truly unsure of what I was going to do about Violet. Sure, our parents were allies, but that treaty would quickly dissolve if Talon found out about me taking his daughter's innocence, war between the two families would be immediate and lives would be lost. I didn't want to risk Violet's safety or that of my family in a war over me having interest in the girl. My eyes drifted to the soft-eyed redhead who gazed at me worriedly, observing how deep in thought that I was. Giving her a small smile, I finished my food and stood before bidding the table goodnight and retiring to my room.

Yes, there were two options for us:

Leave my family and run away with Violet to live in secrecy in fear of our families ever finding us. This option effectively forfeiting my title.

Or, I break things off with her to ensure the treaty stay intact and provide insurance that Violet will be kept safe and away from the dirty part of a mobster's job. But in this option, I would be giving up the person I cared about most.

Chapter 18

Violet

Alphonse Hale gave word to his people that his business trip would be lasting awhile longer. A few days turned into a week, a week turned into two, two weeks turned into three. Nik was suddenly hot and cold, either staying cooped up in his room or attached to my hip; although every night, I felt him crawl into bed with me, wrapping his arms around my waist and pulling me into his chest. This small gesture brought me validation that things were okay on some level, however, his side of my bed would be cold come morning as he would leave my bedroom by dawn. Ravon and Valen were trying to constantly keep me busy with holiday activities as they both noticed the sudden tension around Nik and me. In my brother's mind, he was the first line against my inevitable breakup, promising me that there was plenty more dick in the world. With a slight nod of agreement, I could see that Ravon had his own thoughts, but chose to keep them to himself. I went back to my room early in the evening after a day full of holiday baking, and while I smelled as sweet as a sugar cookie, I was also as sticky as one so I took a quick steamy shower and fell right into bed. I awoke the next morning with the distinct thought of a missing Niklaus. He hadn't come to sleep with me for the first time in what felt like forever, and I tried not to think about how much it bothered me.

I pulled my robe over my body and tightened the tie around my waist. Stuffing my feet into some fuzzy slippers, I opened the door of my bedroom and without looking, slammed into a solid body. Reeling backwards before finding my footing, I gaped at Niklaus' stare that went from my slippers to the messy bun atop my head. The warmth of his gaze shot straight to my core and I bit my lip without realizing, another small gesture not going unnoticed by the hungry looking male.

"Good morning," I said softly, shifting from one foot to the other.

"Dobroye utro malysh [Good morning, baby.]." He replied, his voice low and strained while his eyes blink a few times to focus.

"Is everything okay?" I wondered aloud, leaning against the door frame to appear cool and collected.

"Everything is fine, I just wanted to check on you." His large hand came out to caress my cheek and I leaned into his touch, my eyes fluttering as warmth consumed my belly.

"I'm okay," I whispered softly, feeling him step closer until his lips pressed against mine. I moaned gently into his mouth, lavishing in the warmth of his lips and the taste of mint on his breath. My fingers quickly tangled themselves in Nik's curls, pulling him impossibly closer because I needed him. I needed him in a way that made life without his existence unlivable. But not only did I need him, but I wanted him. I wanted him in a way that the need for his presence was welcomed. I wanted to need him. And I wasn't sure if any of that made sense, but it didn't even matter because...

I am in love with Niklaus. The thought made my throat close around itself because I didn't know what our future held, but I knew that in a world that Talon Maddox rules, I will probably never have a future with Nik. So I kissed him, I kissed him until I felt my feet pushing forward. His back met the wall adjacent to the door and I slowly closed it behind him. A small smirk appeared on his lips, and while my small gesture of dominance seemed to be cute to him, he quickly flipped us around and pressed me firmly between his hard chest and the wall. His slowly came around to feel the curve of my ass before lifting me off the ground and flinging my legs around his waist. I pressed my hips firmly against his, needing a sense of friction against my suddenly swollen sex and moaned in pure ecstasy at the feeling of his erection against my pelvic bone.

"Fuck." He groaned, his fist grabbing a handful of my hair before pulling to expose my throat. Knowing exactly how to make me come undone, Nik zeroed in on the sensitive part of my neck and lavished the area with his tongue, causing my pantie-less sex to gush, my thighs slick with my arousal.

"Please, Daddy, please." I whimpered, grinding my hips forward into his. Nik groaned lowly, one of his hands coming down between my legs to prepare me for his length. Upon feeling my need, he growled in approval, plunging two digits deep into my core. "Ahhh..." I moaned, my hips continuing to roll against his knuckles. Nik opened his mouth to say something, but his jaw quickly snapped shut at the sound of the front door opening and slamming shut. The entire atmosphere shifted and Nik sat me back on the ground, placing his hand over my mouth to instruct me to stay quiet. The house staff had the day off today and Valen was undoubtedly still asleep, Ravon was spending the weekend with Jeremiah which led to one conclusion: there was an unknown person or people in the manor.

"I need you to stay here, I'll handle this and be right back, okay?" Nik pressed a kiss softly against my lips. "Do not move, Violet, I'm not messing around." Without waiting for a reply, Nik stood and exited my room, and all of the sudden, my heart was in my throat. I didn't want him to die because of me.

Niklaus

I had no weapons and I came to accept that whoever had the balls to enter Hale Manor would most definitely have their own, but I would be damned if anything were to happen to Violet. So as I turned the corner, I raised my fists in preparation of a fight, winding my arm back and striking the first thing I came in contact with.

"Ow! What the fuck, Klaus!" A familiar, annoying voice groaned. I took a step back and couldn't help but bite the inside of my cheek to hide my laughter. Archor gripped his gushing nose, blood seeping down this face and onto his shirt. "This is fucking Versace! You owe me a new shirt, ass-hole!"

"You should've called first, how was I supposed to know it was you coming in and not someone else?" I cocked an eyebrow and threw my brother a towel to clean himself up.

"Uh, how about use your goddamn eyes?" Archor growled, tipping his head back while using the towel to clean his face of the blood. I rolled my eyes and leaned against the wall, a painful thought creeping into my mind as I watched him.

"Where's Dad? How long do you think until he comes back home-"

"Look no further, my son." Alphonse Hale appeared from the doorway, several of his armed men surrounding him as he entered. "We were able to finish up the trip just in time to spend the holiday with the family. Where is the little Maddox?"

"Here," A small voice murmured and Violet poked her head out from the hallway, her fuzzy slipper-clad feet padded toward the group of men. "I hope you trip was a successful one." She nodded politely toward my father, a gesture that showed class and grace. Alphonse gave the redhead a warm smile and a gentle nod.

"It was, indeed. Have you had breakfast, Dear?" My father questioned in return. Violet glance from my father to me and then back, shaking her head softly. "Archor, take the girl to the kitchen and prepare her breakfast."

"Father, do you really think that's a good idea-" I tried to amend quickly, feeling a deep rush of possessiveness cloud my judgement.

"We'll be fine!" Archor grinned, throwing an arm around my girl's small shoulders. I held back the urge to growl at my kin, taking a deep breath as I watched them disappear into the dining hall.

"Walk with me, Son." My father smiled slightly and nodded toward the direction of his office. Sighing softly, I stayed to my father's flank until we arrived at his intended destination. Taking a seat at his desk, my father motioned for me to sit and I found myself dropping into a leather chair that faced him. My brain struggled to keep up with the sudden shift of event. One second, I'm about to be nine inches deep in Violet's tight cunt and the next I'm sitting in my father's office? I shook my head in an attempt to keep my thoughts straight.

"You seem stressed, Niklaus." My father stated, leaning back in his chair as he observed me.

"I'm fine." I gave a shrug, trying to put on a mask of indifference.

"How has she been for you, any trouble?" He questioned, cocking an eyebrow.

"Don't you fucking dare leave this room, Violet." I growled, reaching for the knob.

"Yes, Daddy."

"No problems." I shook my head, feeling my palms becoming slick with sweat. I held back the urge to bob my knee up and down with anxiety, knowing I would then be a dead giveaway. My father studied me for a moment, finally breaking his gaze to sigh softly.

"I'm thinking about retiring soon and passing down my title." He leaned back once more, folding his hands in his lap. "But I've gone back and forth for some time, however I was able to finally make my decision when I went on this trip with your brother. Archor was always made for this line of work, he has the passion for it and loves the groundwork. But you... You know how to keep this operation going; you know the books, you know how to delegate, and you have a good head on your shoulder and while I love your brother, his attention is like that of a child. So, when the time is right for me to step down, I will be appointing you to head of the family." My jaw fell slack and I stared at my father. I had always assumed that, because Archor was the eldest, he would be made boss when the time came.

"That's an incredible honor-"

"However," My father interrupted, his eyes trained on me as he spoke. "I can't have you messing up this treaty with Talon Maddox. I saw the way you looked at that girl, Son. Believe it or not, I was your age once too, I know that look."

"I don't know what you mean." I gave a shrug despite the million beats per minute that my heart was pumping.

"She's a beautiful girl, Niklaus and quite special, too. You don't go into our line of work and meet women like Violet often, but this is one tree you don't want to bark up. So I will give you this advice: take the promotion and end whatever it is that is going on with the little Maddox. It will hurt her, it will hurt you, but in the end you will have kept both your family and her family safe. Your mother was the love of my life, but had I known what I now know, I would have never perused her. I never would've-" My father's voice cracked and he closed his eyes, shaking his head softly.

"I don't want to talk about this anymore," I grit my teeth, feeling my eyes begin to well before pushing the emotion away. "I'm not in love with Violet, my job was and is to protect her until she is safe enough to go back to New York. I am honored by the promotion and I thank you for your decision." I stepped toward the door and opened it. "Welcome home, Dad." I slipped out of the room and stalked down the hallway. The first thing on my mind was straightening this situation out once and for all. I had been stupid to think there was any other option than breaking the girl's heart. I should've had more self control. I should've stopped this weeks ago. I shook my head as I got to the door to her room, shoving it open to reveal Archor lounging on Violet's bed as she ate her breakfast.

"Fuck off, Archor." I nodded toward the door and Archor rolled his eyes.

"Violet wants me here-"

"I said FUCK OFF!" I yelled, pointing to the door. The muscle in Archor's jaw flexed as he ground his teeth together, his eyes narrowed at me as he slowly left the room. Shutting the door behind him, I approached the bed. Violet had changed from her robe and into a pair of pink joggers and a white crew neck sweater, she silently picked at the burned pancakes, not lifting her eyes to mine.

"Violet-"

"It's over, isn't it?" She muttered, just loud enough for me to hear. The words struck my heart like a machete, leaving a gushing and festering wound.

"My father has offered me his title after he retires... I can't jeopardize my family or yours for that matter. If your father wasn't Talon Maddox-"

"It's fine," She finally looked up at me, a war of emotions riddled across her face. Her eyes were swimming with unshed tears, however she smiled reassuringly at me. "It had to end sometime, better it's now." I wanted to be happy that she was being so mature about this, I wanted to happy satisfied with the fact this had been a clean break. But I wasn't. I wanted to yell at her to fucking care. I didn't want to see her cry, but the tears would've made me feel as though she were mourning what we had and what we were losing.

I'm losing her.

"Friends?" She tilted her head to the side softly, her smile faltering slightly. She's faking, she's not happy and she's barely keeping it together. I felt my eyes begin to prickle and I quickly turned away from her so she wouldn't see them well.

"Yeah." I nodded, walking to the door.

Friends.

Chapter 19

V iolet

Ravon stared at me in shock, his jaw slack with surprise as he handed me two aspirin. I popped the pills into my mouth and knocked them back with a gulp of water; yes, my brain hurt and yes, I was struggling. It had been a full day since Niklaus and I ended things between us and when I woke up with a raging headache and swollen eyes from the ocean of tears I had shed, Ravon rushed to my rescue. He pulled me into a tight embrace and rubbed my back gently, the urge to cry becoming apparent at the feeling of my throat tightening.

"Babe, it'll be okay... I never thought he would actually... You two are-" He shook his head, not sure of what to say, "I'm so sorry, Lottie." I hugged him back softly and pulled away, a stray tear falling down my cheek. Ravon's thumb came out to catch the liquid before taking my hands in his and kissing my knuckles. "I know just what you need."

Ravon pulled me into the bathroom where he quickly put himself to work, setting up small tables with nail polish, facial masks, pore cleanser pads, wax and waxing strips all while drawing me a bath. Instructing me to strip, I absentmindedly pulled my clothes off and slid into the hot water, letting the liquid saturate my skin and work at my toughened muscled. Without realizing my eyes had closed, a soft 'plop' sound erupted from the water and I popped open one eye to see where it had come from. Ravon had thrown a rose petal bath bomb into the water and I hummed in appreciation, closing my eye to join its twin in some much needed relaxation. Ravon let me soak in the water until it was nearly temped before urging me out of the tub. Wrapping a plush bathrobe around me, he sat me on the edge of the tub and began giving me a Christmas-themed pedicure and matching manicure. My fingers and toes had everything from Santa and elves, to pine trees and snowflakes. With Ray's distraction, I felt somewhat better and even mustered up a smile. By the afternoon, we had indulged in a marathon of 80' movies. We were a quarter way through Weird Science when my landline rang. Cocking my eyebrows in surprise, I picked up the phone.

"Redhead, is that you?" A slightly familiar voice sounded.

"Who is this?" I questioned as Ravon leaned against the phone to listen on with me.

"It's Bash, but I've only got another minute before they kick me off your line. I'm throwing a Christmas Eve party tonight. I want you there. I'll send Klaus the address, come in something Christmas-y!" The line went dead and Ravon and I exchanged looks.

"Babe, you've got plans tonight!" Ray suddenly gush, rushing to my closet to pull out all of my red, green, silver, and gold dresses. My fingers twisted at each other in anxiety as Niklaus' face popped into my head.

"But Nik would be going as well-" Ray suddenly stopped, striding over to me quickly and taking my chin between his index finger.

"Niklaus Hale is nobody to you anymore. He stupidly ended things with a fine female with a beautiful mind, his loss; thank you, next!" He kissed my forehead, "Now let's make him drool and have some fun."

I shifted uneasily, my heels clicking with the movement of my legs. Ravon's fingers were linked with mine as he pulled me in front of Niklaus' bedroom door. With his free hand, Ravon knocked hard on the door and took a step back to distance himself. The door swung open and I felt my brain swarm with the familiarity of Nik's rugged features and warm cologne. I attempted a look of confidence, lifting my chin at the feeling of his eyes finding me.

"What's up? Why're you two dressed up?" He questioned, his voice thick with a familiar accent of lust.

"Have you not checked your phone? Violet's been invited to Sebastian Coleman's Christmas Eve party. We need a ride." Ravon said, crossing his arms over his chest. Nik's eyebrows cocked in surprise and confusion.

"And you want to go to this party under no one's influenced?" He looked between my best friend and me unconvinced.

"Yeah, I figured: why not?" I gave a shrug and looked to my left, feeling heated under his watchful gaze. The three of us stood for a long time, I think Nik wasn't sure what to say. We were in a weird place now, forced to see each other despite having ended our relationship. Painful and reoccurring.

"No." He finally replied, moving to shut his door. A flare of anger ripped through my spine and shoved my shoe in the door, stopping him from completely shutting it. Cocking an eyebrow at me, Nik pulled the door open to accommodate me.

"I'm allowed to have some fun." I grit, my jaw flexing slightly in the midst of my irritation. Nik frowned and stepped forward, his chest touching mine with the close proximity. I gasped softly, the anger flushing from my system and quickly shifting to shock and somehow arousal. Get your shit together, Violet, c'mon!

"As much as I enjoy this bold attitude," His eyes drifted my lips for a moment before returning to my irises. "I said no." He took a quick step back and shut the door behind himself. I stood staring at the door for a moment. Ravon's hands appeared on my waist and he turned me around.

"Plan B." He shrugged, gently shoving me further down the hallway. Ravon's backup plan was yet another Hale man who was perfectly fine taking me to Sebastian Coleman's party. The ride to the Coleman residence was filled with rap music that was extremely loud, vibrating the seats of his sleek red car. When we finally pulled up to the mansion, I felt a rush of anxiety and noticing this, Ray rubbed my shoulders. "It's going to be okay, let's have a couple drinks and dance like there's no tomorrow. Then we'll go right back to the manor, let's just let go for a bit." He offered me a reassuring smile and I returned it softly, allowing him to lead me from the car.

"Just find me whenever you're ready to go home," Archor winked before setting off into the party. I remembered the ballroom well, but the decor had changed from that of a sleek business get together to a wild and vibrant Christmas party. Lavishly decorated Christmas trees were placed in front of the many long windows that gave way to the scenery of the city. Green, red, and white strobe lights fluttered across the room as the heavy bass coming from the speaker system; long strings of glittery garland were hung both and high low, giving an iridescent glow to the room; the bartender and all of the waiters and waitresses were dressed in tuxedos and sequin-covered dresses, adding to the high scale atmosphere. Ray squealed at my right, hooking his elbow around mine and pulling me toward the beautiful lit bar, ordering me a spiked eggnog. I took a long drink and hummed at the creamy taste, barely tasting the alcohol on my tongue.

"Let's go dance our asses off!" Ray through his hands in the air and I giggled, following him onto the dance floor. A pair of hands found my waist, pulling me into a hard chest. I closed my eyes I thought about Niklaus; his large hands splayed across my hips, guiding me against this body in gyrated movements. But this wasn't Nik and I knew that the moment the man's hands touched my body, but I ignored the urge to flee away from the unknown male and danced like I didn't care. My hips rolled to the beat, feeling absolutely at the top of my game as one of my favorite rappers came through the speakers. People were beginning to watch me, but I didn't care. After Nik ended things, it felt like I wasn't good enough or even worth his trouble, so it was nice to feel sexy and admired in the moment.

If Nik didn't want me, fine, then I was going to find someone who did.

Niklaus

I knocked gently on Violet's door, a cup of hot cocoa in my hand. My pulse was racing with the thought of seeing her; she was so angry with me earlier, part of me felt sort of guilty and another part of me thought it was pretty fucking cute. I waited... I waited. Tapping my foot impatiently on the ground, I knocked harder. Is she really that mad at me? What happened to being friends? I waited five more minutes before I had enough, I typed the security code into the control panel and opened the door, dropping the cup of molten chocolate onto the hardwood. The room was empty, bed still made from the maid staff earlier in the evening. It's eleven o' clock at night, where the fuck was she? My brain quickly shifted gears and I turned on my heel, running down the hall. I checked the gym, the dining hall, the in-home theater, and all other rooms that I doubted she had ever been in.

"Fucking hell." I knocked on Archor's door and waited… and waited. Grabbing the handle, I pushed the door open and my jaw clenched at the sight. Lights off, empty bed. Wherever Archor was… I had a feeling Violet wasn't far away. Sprinting through the halls, I whipped open the door to my office and quickly punched in the password to enter my computer. Accessing our GPS system, I quickly tracked down the coordinates of Archor's car and growled lowly when I realized his whereabouts. I logged out of my system and grabbed my keys from the hook on the wall before locking up my office. Making my way through the manor, I jogged down the steps into the underground garage where my car was parked. As soon as I was situated, I pressed the button of the garage opener and sped out, my tires squealing against the concrete. I whipped through the streets of Chicago, my anger bubbling and bubbling, my breathing heavy and erratic. I'm going to kill him. The redhead is going to pay for this, she is in so much fucking trouble. I parked right outside the stairway of the Coleman residence. Locking the vehicle, I ignored the bellhop and strode up the long stairway leading to the mansion four steps at a time.

Yes, I was getting sickly excited at the thought of the redhead's face. She would be shocked to see me. Did she think she'd get away with this little break-out? Did she think I wouldn't notice. Oh, she had another thing coming. When I finally made it inside, I zeroed in on Archor and ground my teeth together. Making my way through the crowd, I grabbed him by the back of the shirt and pulled him backward. The girl he had been talking to squealed in surprise and I spun my brother around to face me.

"Where the fuck is she?" I growled and despite the loud music, Archor knew what I had said and pointed into the crowded dance floor. Letting go of him, I felt him put some serious distance between us as I peered through the large group of people. My eyes found her hair first, shining against the strobe lights like artificial fire. But when I saw the rest of her, my hands curled into fists, my eyesight went red, my blood boiled. The redhead was in the outfit she had sported earlier: a white silk blouse tucked into a green sequined skirt that ended mid-thigh, paired with sliver heels; however, she wasn't alone. Some idiot frat boy had his hands on her hips, grinding her backside into his crotch as they dance together.

"Oh shit." A familiar voice said from behind me. I recognized the voice to belong Ravon and made a mental note to deal with him later, but for now, I couldn't take my eyes off of the blond touching my girl. I zigzagged through the crowd, coming up from behind them to avoid ruining the delicious surprised face Violet would undoubtedly sport too quickly. Grabbing the back of the frat boy's shirt, I pulled him backward and reveled in the moment he made a slight choking noise. When he hit the floor with an audible 'oof,' I stood behind Violet as she slowly realized her partner was gone. When she finally turned to face me, the smile she had been wearing quickly disappeared into an expression of sheer horror.

"Nik," She gasped, slowly putting her hands up in surrender. "W-What're you doing here?"

"What am I doing here? Violet, what the fuck are you doing here? I told you no, little girl." I pulled her chin between my index finger and thumb, biting my lip softly. "You are under my supervision and what I say goes." She pulled away from me, an angry frown set on her lips.

"You don't own me, Niklaus." She pointed at me angrily and spun on her heel, taking off in the other direction. I flinched slightly at the sound of her using my full name. It took me a moment to realize she had walked away and just as I was about to go after her, a stupid grinning face appeared in front of me.

"Man, you made it!" Bash slapped my back, hooking his arm around my shoulders.

"Why the fuck did you invite Violet?" I yelled, pulling away from him. His brow furrowed in confusion, trying to come up with an answer.

"I thought you two were into each other? You made out on my balcony last time, I figured you guys had shacked up by now." I stared at him in disbelief, pulling him toward the bar for a less crowded conversation.

"How did you know we made out? Who have you told?" I seethed, a mixture of rage and confusion washing through me.

"No one; dude, we have cameras everywhere: of course I knew you guys made out. Honestly, I had no idea it would be such a big deal." I sighed softly and shook my head, letting out a pent up breath I had held too long.

"We hooked up and I had to end things; my father is promoting me when he retires, and I couldn't risk the treaty with Talon Maddox. Now things are weird between us and I don't know how to act around her." I clenched my jaw at the memory of Violet with the frat boy.

"Fuck, Klaus, if I would've known, I never would've..." Bash shook his head, giving me a side hug.

"No worries, man. I was trying to keep it on the down low, seeing as who her father is." I felt a headache coming on, but I couldn't focus on that. "What should I do, Bash?"

"Do you care about her?" He questioned, "I mean, beyond fucking?"

"Of course." I couldn't help but roll my eyes.

"If you found out she were with someone else, would you be okay with that?" I stared at him for a moment, feeling my heart sink at the mere thought.

"No." I replied simply, my head dropping slightly with sorrow.

"Do you love her?" He cocked an eyebrow, his voice a solution of intrigue and shock. The term had never entered my brain until this moment. My eyes scanned the room for her, but I didn't have to see her to know it, I didn't even have to think about it.

"I-" I stopped before I could say another word, my eyes had finally found her. The frat boy had reemerged and found a secluded spot with Violet. He placed one hand on her hip and the other danced across her collarbone; he was going to kiss her. I jolted forward and plowed through the dense crowd, not bothering weave or allow people to move out of my way. Their lips were milometers apart when I arrived in front of them, Violet's eyes were beginning to flutter closed in anticipation.

"Back the fuck off." I shoved his shoulder and Violet's eyes shot open, zeroing in on me like a target.

"Hey, you're the guy who shoved me earlier; what the fuck is your problem, bro?" He puffed out his chest, obviously trying to put on a show to impress Violet. I rolled my eyes.

"Move." I stepped around him, "What are you trying to do, Violet? Do you want me to start killing people?" She crossed her arms across her chest.

"Stop it, Nik. You have no reason to start killing people-"

"If they touch you, I have more than enough reason to kill someone." I growled, feeling my hands ball into fists.

"No, you don't. You gave that up, Nik, I never asked for this." She shoved my gently, trying to move away from me. I became a wall, not allowing her to move past me. "Move, Nik." Someone grabbed my left shoulder, swinging me around.

"I wasn't finished talking, bro." He began measure me up, "Now it's obvious this girl doesn't want you around, so I say you get the fuck away before I make you." I smirked slightly, stepping forward until his nose was practically touching my collarbone.

"You even attempt get between me and my girl, I'll fucking end you and you obviously don't know who you're fucking with, boy. Everyone knows a Hale knows where to hide a body." His eyes went wide with fear a moment before I cocked my head backward and headbutted him square in the fore-head, turning around to face Violet once more.

"Are you going to come easily or are you going to make this hard?" I cocked my head to the side in challenge, smirking slightly at the sound of the frat boy's body hitting the floor. Before I could blink Violet bee-lined for refuge in Ravon's direction, but knowing her well enough, I lurched forward to catch her wrist before she could get any farther. She thrashed and beat her small fists against my chest, Sebastian sent me a double thumbs up as he watched us head upstairs toward the private wing.

Chapter 20

Violet

"Let me go right now, Niklaus!" This only seemed to encourage the man, throwing me over his shoulder like a light sack of potatoes. I squirmed and punched his butt as hard as I could.

"Fuck Violet, quit it!" He demanded, opening a door to his right and carrying me within. I stumbled slightly as he placed me back on my feet and I blinked a few times to refocus my attention on how angry I was with the man in front of me. Without thinking, I wound my hand backward and slapped him across the face.

"You're being a dick, you had no right to make me come up here!" His face, now sporting a red tinge across his cheek, remained indifferent despite my assault. "I'm out of here." I attempted to move around him, only for him to block the door.

"Going back to frat boy downstairs?" He tilted his head slightly to the left, half a challenge and half curiosity.

"For your information, Tyler is in law school, which is more than I can say about you." I tipped my chin up confidently, crossing my arms over my chest.

"Seriously?" He took a step forward, making me take a step back. "Is that what he told you he's going to school for? That tool wouldn't even know how to get to a college, much less attend." Nik took another step forward and I swallowed thickly as I took a step backward. "How did it feel when he touched you?" I felt the wall against my back as I took another step behind me, Niklaus closed the distance between us, his fingers just barely grazing my side as his hand made its way up my body.

"Wouldn't you like to know." I mumbled, trying to remain in charge of the conversation. His hand was against my throat, his thumb brushing over my pulse as he dipped his head into the nape of my neck. His warm breath fanned across the sensitive skin and my body shuddered.

"I hate to break it to you, baby girl, but no one can make you feel good like I can," His lips brushed against the sweet spot of my neck and my back arched, making my chest press against his. "No one knows your body like I do," Nik's tongue circled the tender area and I whimpered, my knees wobbling slightly as I felt the familiar swarm of arousal begin to infiltrate my brain. Reality was quick to catch up and I used all of my strength to push him away. Nik took a few steps back while

I scurried to the other side of the room, trying to put some distance between us so my brain could operate normally.

"What are you doing? You ended things with me, Nik, you can't just pick and choose-"

"And what if I don't want things to end, Violet?" He took a step toward me, his face falling into an expression of helplessness and anger. "All decisions I make are in the name of your safety-"

"When are you, my father, and everyone else going to realize I don't need constant protection? I can make my own decisions, I can handle myself!" I threw my hands up in frustration. "I'm not a child, Niklaus; my father does not run my life. I choose what my future looks like and who I spend it with."

"So you would give up everything," He motioned around the room, "Your family, the luxury of this lifestyle, the money... all for me." He stated questioningly, his voice laced with disbelief.

"None of that matters when you're with the one you love," I strode forward, pushing him away from the only exit. "But stupid me, right? Falling in love with a ruthless gangster who would choose this lifestyle and the money over me." I reached for the door only for a large hand to wrap around my wrist, pulling me back. I stared up at him angrily, wanting to scream at him that he was an asshole, to punch him in his outrageously good-looking face. But I didn't. He looked down at me, his eyes practically bursting with emotion as he cupped my cheeks.

"Say it again," He whispered softly. My heart was suddenly hammering in my chest and I struggled to keep myself from drowning in his chocolate eyes.

"I'm stupid?" I replied, unknowingly keeping in tune with his volume.

"Try again," He rolled his eyes and I couldn't help but smile slightly.

"I love you," I amended and before I could end the sentence with his name, his lips were on mine. His kiss was desperate and hungrily, like he were starved and unwilling to share. His hands grasped my hips and suspended me in the air, his fingers securing themselves on my ass to hold me up. Our kiss was never broken and even though I could feel him walking, I felt as though I were floating on a cloud. My head lulled with the satisfaction of Nik's lips on mine and my body hummed with the familiarity of his touch. I was gently pressed into the soft sheets of the bed below me, Nik hovered over my body and sucked on my bottom lip in request. Parting my lips, I welcomed his tongue in my mouth and moaning as it massaged my own.

"Say it again," He mumbled against my now swollen lips.

"I love you." I moaned softly, feeling his fingers trace down to the beginning of my skirt before pulling the blouse from beneath it. The soft fabric was ripped from my body in the next second, the red lacy bra I had put on earlier presenting my bust like an unopened Christmas gift. Nik growled in approval and kissed down my cleavage, his teeth unhooking the clasp between my breast. The bra popped open and reveal my breast to the cool air, my nipples instantly pebbling under his appraising stare.

"So fucking beautiful," He murmured, swallowing quickly before dipping his head down and capturing my left bud in his mouth. Nik's teeth grazed the sensitive flesh and my back arched, pushing my nipple further into his mouth. His hands were back on my hips and pressing them back into the bed as I squirmed beneath him. Moving to my opposite nipple, Nik was quick to give his utmost attention to the neglected globe. My core began to pool and I felt my thong become slick with my arousal. I attempted to pull down my skirt, but Nik was quick to slap my hands away. "Skirt stays on." His lips kissed down my chest and then I was suddenly flipped on my stomach, my ass high in the air as Nik positioned me on my knees with my face pressed against the sheets. Audibly gasping, my eyes rolled in the back of my head as Niklaus wasted no time, his tongue plunging into my sex while he lathered two of this fingers in my wetness. I cried out, the pleasure of his mouth shooting directly to my core.

"Daddy!" I whined, my voice sounding something between erotic and demanding.

"Don't worry, baby girl, my cock will be buried to the hilt inside your sweet pussy soon enough, just be patient." Without any warning, Niklaus' finger were pumping inside of me, curling against my g-spot to achieve my loudest scream yet. Now on his back, Nik wiggled his head between my legs as if he were a mechanic checking out the underside of a car before his tongue was lapping against my clit. The combination of his fingers and tongue made my vision go starry, my orgasm taking over my body. My entire being shook with the pleasure of my climax, only for Nik to strip of his clothing and flip me back on my back. Throwing my legs over his shoulders, my skirt was completely hiked up and covered my stomach. I was still recovering for my orgasm when he pressed the tip of his cock against my opening. My mouth developed the shape of an 'o' as he slowly slid his member into me and just as promised, he buried himself as deeply inside of me as was physically possible.

"Say it again, baby girl." He demanded, not moving an inch until the words left my lips.

"I love you, Niklaus-" Before I could finish, Nik completely withdrew from my sex before plunging back in. Lifting my hips up to a better angle, the male drilled into me like a crazed animal, his eyes remaining on my own, making sure he didn't miss a moment of my pleasurable experience. One of his hands came out to assist in preparation of my next climax, his thumb rubbing rhythmically at my clit with each of his thrust.

"You're mine, Violet, say it."

"I'm yours, Nik, I'm yours." I whimpered, my vision clouding once again. Realizing I was close, Nik pulled out of me and sat on the bed, pulling me on top of him. I sank down the length of his dick and we hummed in unison at the euphoric sensation. I moved my hips up and down, my breasts bouncing with each movement. Nik's lips recaptured mine, this time kissing me slowly. My hips rocked against his, the tip of his cock twitched inside of me and not soon after, he broke the kiss to thrust into my sex from beneath me. I met each of his thrusts, earning growls of approval from his lips as he neared his own orgasm.

"So fucking close," His eyes pinched closed as he thrust harder and faster into me. My eyes squeezed shut as my second climax hit me like a train, my sex clenching around Nik's cock, pushing him over the edge. His seed spilled into my core and I hummed at the fullness as the liquid filled me. I slid off of Nik's lap and slumped at his side, the only sounds being the gentle hum from the music downstairs and our erratic breathing. Nik pulled me to his chest, kissing my forehead gently as we came down from our climaxes.

"I missed you," He whispered softly, his fingertips tracing patterns on my back as we laid together.

"I missed you, too." I couldn't help but smile against him, feeling the familiar feeling of butterflies fluttering in my belly.

"What do you say to going home and spending Christmas Eve together the right way?" Nik swung his leg over me and gently pressed his lips to my nose, then my lips, down my neck and peppered little kisses against my collarbones.

"Yes!" I giggled softly, squirming from beneath him before falling off the bed. I collected my bra and blouse from the floor before putting them back on. Niklaus slowly got up and pulled on his own clothes before collecting his keys from the floor and placing them in his pocket. I checked myself in the mirror once more before accepting Nik's outstretched hand, allowing him to lead me out of the room. We descended from the stairs and made our way outside to Nik's car. The ride back to the manor was quiet, but comfortable. Things felt normal again and Nik seemed to be incapable of keeping his hands off of me, whether it be his hand on my knee as he drove or a sweet kiss at a red light. We arrived back at the manor and Nik parked his car in the underground garage. Niklaus linked our fingers as we walked down the halls to my bedroom and once we arrived, I peeled the tight clothes from my body. Pulling off his shirt, Nik offered the the article of clothing and I slipped it over my head. We settled into bed and I became a little spoon, burrowing into the warm chest of the man I loved.

Chapter 21

My eyes peeled open the next morning, my right hand feeling for the warm body that had been sleeping next to me all night. Instead of meeting skin, I felt the cool presence of a cardboard box. Turning with curiosity, a grin spread across my face as I took in the sight of the wrapped gift. A small paper name tag hung from the large red bow set neatly in the center of the top of the box.

For my Babygirl.

My heart nearly skipped as the note's content reverberated around my skull. Pulling the wrapping paper away from the gift, I ripped open the box and pulled the two pieces of fabric from the bottom. My eyes traveled over the pajama set that had traditional red and white winter print, paired with fluffy white faux fur slippers. Grinning widely as I stretched, I collected my gift in my hands and headed toward the bathroom. Pulling off my clothes, I stepped into the shower and lathered my body in a strawberry scented body wash before massaging coconut shampoo into my hair. After washing the soap off, I turned the knob of the shower off and squeezed the excess water from my hair. I wrapped a warm towel around myself and stepped into my new slippers that I had placed just outside the tub. After I had shaved my legs, brushed my teeth and properly dried off, I pulled the ensemble on and glanced at myself in the mirror.

Adding a touch of makeup to my face, I was just about to start toward the exit of my bedroom when the door began to open. My heart fluttered with the possibility of seeing Niklaus, the mere idea of his eyes sweeping up my body like the always did made my core clench with need.

"Good morning Daddy-" My heart stopped, my mouth going try as I realized who had actually entered my room.

"Good morning, my little Lottie, how did you know it was me?" My father grinned, both amused and confused by my shocked expression.

"I- Uh-" I stumbled with my words, my heart beating rapidly in my chest, but for an entirely different reason. Did Nik know my father would be coming today, is that why he left my bedroom so early?

"Princess?" My father questioned, stepping forward to take my hand in his. "Is everything okay?" I nodded quickly and squeezed his hand gently, a lopsided smile on my face as I tried to cover up my anxiety.

"Of course, I'm just so happy to see you!" I beamed, throwing my arms around his neck in a tight hug. Despite the tension building within me, I relaxed into my father's embrace, the very same one that had protected me all of my life. The deep scent of sandalwood and cigars, the comfort of his soft cotton v-neck, his strong arms wrapped around my small frame. I closed my eyes and reveled in the familiarity of our hug.

"What the fuck!" Another masculine voice sounded from behind us, the very one that I had intended my initial greeting for. My father and I separated, and he placed me behind him. "Oh shit." Nik realized who the man in front of him was, his face going pale. "Talon Maddox."

"And who are you?" My father growled, his hand on the glock on his hip, preparing for whatever was to happen next. I placed my hand on my fathers, shaking my head as he glanced my way for a mere second.

"Niklaus Hale," The younger man announced, "I meant no harm, I just didn't expect to see you here and at first glance, I didn't know who you were." My father visibly relaxed and he gave an appreciative nod.

"Than you father picked the right man for the job of protecting my daughter," My father held out his hand to Nik, "For that, I am deeply thankful." Nik slowly reached for my father's hand, not exactly trusting the situation yet, but once their palms met, my father gave his a firm shake. Niklaus looked to me, his eyes trying to communicate with me, but my brain was still trying to grasp the fact my father was here in the flesh. Tension was thick within the room and knowing my father, he could feel it too. "Is there something going on-"

"Lottie! Lottie!" Valen burst into the room; his eyes wild with intent, hair tufted to the side from a restful sleep. "Dad's-" I sent him a pleading look, but his eyes quickly moved from my father, to me, and then to Niklaus who was still looking peckish. Val's eyes finally met mine once more and I plead with him, from behind my father, to play it cool. "-Got a surprise for you." My father scoffed, shoving Valen's shoulder playfully.

"Way to ruin the theatrics of a surprise, but that'll have to wait until dinner. Right now, I need some Lottie time." My father lifted me from the floor and spun us around, a peaceful smile on his face as he sat me back on my feet. Nik leaned against the wall, not hearing or seeing what was happening in front of him. It was obvious that the wheels in Nik's head were turning, but I couldn't exactly figure out what he may be thinking. It's one thing to hear about Talon Maddox, but to be in the presence of him, gravity is a lot heavier; air is thicker to breathe. My father's fingers were around my wrist in the next moment, pulling me through the door of my bedroom and pulling me down the hall.

"Dad, where are we going?" I felt my heart beat faster and faster. If he is here in Chicago, did that mean it was safe to go home? My body ached with the idea of never seeing Niklaus again.

"Dad?" My father cocked an eyebrow. "You've never called me Dad, it's always been Daddy." My father continued to pull me, but his tone was slightly lower, almost as if my new variation of his title had hurt him in some way.

"Well, I'm nineteen, don't you think I'm getting a little old-" My father stopped, cupping my cheeks in his had as he bore down at me, his eyes lit on fire.

"From the time you left your mother's body to the day you die an old woman, you will be my little girl, understand me, leasleanbh [little girl]?" He questioned, his Irish accent thick as he spoke down to me.

"Yes Sir," I gave a gentle nod and my father turned the corner, letting me go from his grasp just as three pairs of hands pulled me into a tight hug. I squealed as Vaughn, Viktor, and Vinny enveloped me in a loving embrace.

"Little sister! It's been far too long, you've grown at least two inches-" Vinny chuckled.

"We brought gifts, but open mine first, the other lads got you nothing but shit, you know I know you best." Vik grabbed my chin affectionately and gently pinched my nose. I grinned and smiled up at my quiet older brother Vaughn who had stayed silent, but kept a protective arm around my shoulder.

"I missed you, too, Vaughn." I giggled and hugged them all close.

"What about me?" Valen cursed from behind us and the four of us open our arms, accepting our final sibling into this familial huddle. A throat cleared from across the room and I poked my head out of the group of redheads, my eyes zeroing in on the beautiful woman in front of me.

"Mom!" I yelled, a wide grin across my lips as I expertly slithered out of the tight grips of my brothers to embrace my mother. She cupped my cheeks and kissed my forehead, tears welling in her eyes.

"My girl, how have you been?" She whispered softly, placing her forehead against mine.

"I've been fine, great actually," I assured her, squeezing her with glee. We separated, by our fingers stayed entwined. I looked around the room of Maddox's and felt my heart swell with contentment, but as I panned all the way to the left, my eyes met with Niklaus'. Suddenly reality was set back into place and I realized I was not the same girl that I had been back in New York. A lot has happened in the few months I had stayed with the Hale's and I didn't intend on going back to the sheltered girl I had been before.

"Maddox's, what a wonderful surprise and a Merry Christmas to you all," Alphonse Hale spoke and we all turned toward our host. "Hot cocoa and fresh, warm coffee cake will be offered in the sitting room, along with all of the presents brought by our guests and a few of my own family's. I slowly took my father's hand, allowing him to lead me toward the sitting room, however my eyes never left Nik's. He trailed behind my family while Archor talked his ear off of about some girl he had bedded the night before and shooed off before everyone awoke. I sat on a love seat next to the beautifully lit Christmas tree that had been put up by the staff yesterday. Everyone tore through their presents within twenty minutes, but I had little interest in opening gifts. I could feel Nik's eyes flicker to me every so often and it took my everything not to rush to Alphonse Hale in a panic.

I don't want to leave, please let me stay!

One last gift sat under the and everyone's eyes snapped to it as the box moved all by itself. Several guns were suddenly lifted from holsters and other hiding places, but Niklaus quickly stood up, holding his hands up to the armed men in the room to put their firearms away.

"It's nothing harmful, just a gift for Violet, it's from me and Archor." Nik slid the box over to me as Archor cocked an eyebrow in confusion.

"I didn't get her a gif-" Nik must've hurt Archor in warning somehow, because Archor's stopped talking mid-sentence and instead grimaced in pain. "Oh, I remember now, Merry Christmas Violet."

"Thank you," I smiled softly, my only on Niklaus as I pulled the ribbon undone from the top. I finally broke away from Nik's gaze to cautiously open the box. Small scratching sounds erupted from the box and I prepared myself for the worst, but as the top of the box came off, my heart melted within my chest. "Oh my god." I breathed out in pure disbelief.

"What is it?" Vaughn questioned, stretching a bit to peek inside. I reached into the box, my fingers coming into contact with its soft fur as I picked up the small being and held it to my chest.

"He's an American Eskimo, I remember you once told me your grandmother had had one when you were little." Nik replied softly as I inspected the little outfit the puppy was wearing, one that matched the pajama set he had left for me to wear this morning, the very same set that I was currently sporting. "I thought he could keep you company while you stayed with us."

"You're welcome." Archor sent me a wink and leaned back in his chair, but the small flirtatious act hadn't gone unnoticed by my father, whose jaw set tightly and flexed from beneath the skin of his cheeks.

"Thank you... So much." I tried to contain my emotions, but I couldn't help my eyes as they began to well.

"Are you okay, Sweetie?" My mother asked from my side, squeezing my shoulder gently.

"Yeah," I nodded, wiping away my tears, "I'm just so glad you could all be here today." I amended my true statement, because this puppy was meant to keep me company during my stay at Hale Manor, but with my father being her, it was unlikely that my stay would be for much longer. "What's his name?" I looked to Niklaus who had an ashen expression on his face.

"I thought I'd leave that up to you," He replied, "Although, I've been calling him Bear. I've been hiding him in my room for the past two days and he's a terrible bed-hog and is kind of an asshole when he's tired, kinda like a Bear, but feel free to call him whatever you want. The lady from the rescue named him Hercules, but I didn't think that fit him well." I grinned softly, the tears that had welled in my eyes now falling down my cheeks.

"I like the name Bear, it's perfect." I kissed the top of my puppy's head and held him close, smiling as he delivered several kisses across my face.

"Hey Hale, how big will that thing get? Is this a kind of dog she could fit in her purse?" Vinny questioned, rubbing the puppy's head affectionately.

"I think he'll be somewhere around twenty-five pounds when he's an adult." Nik shrugged, leaning back against the sofa. The day flew by quickly and as expected, my father never let me out of his sight. From watching Christmas movies to hanging out with Ravon, my father was not far away. When it got to be later in the afternoon, I was finally able to excuse myself to change into something nicer for Christmas dinner. My brain ached from the amount of time I spent trying to figure out a plan, but without several major details, it was hard to settle on anything concrete. Was my father here temporarily or was he here to take me home? Did Nik even want something long-term, I mean, I told him I loved him several times last night and he never once reciprocated. I shook my head as I changed into a mid-thigh length sparkly long-sleeved red dress, curling my hair until I felt it looked presentable before applying some eyeliner and mascara.

"You look beautiful," A voice stated from behind me and I turned, feeling my heart flutter at Nik's presence.

"I didn't even hear you come in," I smiled, reaching for Bear who was situated in Nik's large arms. Bear eagerly leaped toward me and snuggled his small head into the nape of my neck.

"Go figure, he's in love with you," Nik chuckled, rubbing the puppy's back gently. After a few moments of silence, his fingers came out to cradle my chin, his dark brown irises boring into mine.

"Whatever happens, I'm going to make sure you stay with me," He pressed a soft kiss to my forehead, "I left your room this morning to put Bear in the box for you to open, but by the time I got back..." He shook his head. "I thought we'd have more time."

"Me too," I sighed softly, leaning my forehead against his chest. The pressurized door to my room began to open again and we quickly separated from each other. I busied myself by putting little Bear on his new fluffy dog bed which was full of vibrantly color squeaky toys.

"Violet, are you ready for dinner- Oh, Niklaus, I didn't expect you to be here," My father said as his eyes fell on the man who'd been watching over me these past few months.

"Yes, well, I thought I would escort your daughter to the dining hall." Nik gave a soft shrug and my father gave a curt nod.

"Great minds, do in fact, think alike. I had the same idea." My father reached for my hand. "Dinner is nearly ready, Lottie, let's get going." I bit the inside of my cheek, placing my hand in my father's before letting him lead me from my bedroom. Nik followed us out and shut the bedroom door behind himself. The short walk to the dining hall felt like it lasted forever, but when we finally arrived, the entirety of the two families (along with Ravon) had found their seats at the dining table. My father pulled out a chair for me to sit down and scooted me into the table before taking his place beside me. Niklaus was able to get a seat directly across from me, much to my relief as my father was beginning to annoy me with his constant watchfulness.

Dinner was served with three options: a ham entree with a side of potatoes and gravy, garlic roasted asparagus, and a cheese baked crescent roll; a roasted beef entree with a side of garlic buttered mashed potatoes, baked Brussels sprouts, and brown sugar roasted carrots; and finally, a rotisserie chicken entree with bacon fried green beans, baked garlic fingerling potatoes with a biscuit on the side. Once everyone had ordered, the large group began talking. My father and Alphonse Hale talked business in hushed tones, Archor was connecting well with Viktor and Vinny while Ravon talked with Valen and Vaughn about the upcoming Spring trends coming through on the most recent fashion catwalk. The food arrived a short time later, as the kitchen staff had been preparing the meals all throughout the day in anticipation for this moment. The chef came out to ask how the food was and my mother was quick to gain his attention, asking for his recipes on everything on the menu for the evening. I picked at my food, despite the ache of my hunger. I'm going to eat a million more meals, but I couldn't bear the thought of eating another breakfast, lunch, or dinner without Nik sitting at the same table.

"Is something wrong with your food, leasleanbh?" My father questioned, noticing my lack of appetite. I shook my head and glanced at the middle of the table, searching for an excuse.

"It just needs a bit of salt, could you please hand me the salt shaker, Dad-" I watched my father grimace at the shortened name and quickly amended: "Daddy?" My father gave a gentle nod, approving of my shift in word before reaching for the shaker. I was about to sigh in relief, if not for the moment my father's hand met Niklaus' in the middle of the table. No, my lungs ceased to breathe in that moment. The whole room went silent in that moment. Because in that moment, Niklaus had responded to the name Daddy and reached to hand me the salt shaker, causing his fingers to meet my father's at the center of the table. This was not good. As I slowly turned my head to face my father, his face was an expression of rage and murder, but his eyes were not on me. They were on the man who called himself my Daddy.

Chapter 22

"Would someone please explain to me what is going on?" Alphonse Hale was the first to speak, but this did not help with the tension in the room. Archor was squirming in his seat beside his father, a mixture of emotion written on his face, ready to burst at any moment.

"This is probably some sort of misunderstanding, Klaus was just trying to be polite and hand Violet the salt since he was closer to it than Mr. Maddox, right Niklaus?" Ravon cocked an eyebrow, urging Nik to go along with him. My father was trembling in the seat beside me, his anger reaching new points as Niklaus stared back at him, an unwavering sense of confidence and ease radiating from the younger man, as if he weren't afraid of anything.

"Son, please inform our esteemed guest that you do not have relations with his daughter." Alphonse said, his tone almost pleading. Nik's jaw ticked and I felt my heart drop into my stomach. This isn't happening. This isn't happening-

"I'm sorry you had to find out like this-" Before Niklaus could finish, my father stood straight up, knocking the chair he had been sitting on to the floor with a loud knock. My father drew the glock from his hip and pointed it on Niklaus, an angry growl escaping my lips. But Nik was quick to respond, drawing out his own gun and pointing it at my father's direction. No one in the room knew what to do except for gasp. These were two important members between the two families, who do you protect without angering the other side? The treaty between the Maddox's and the Hale's was hanging on by a thread."-Reconsider what you're doing Talon, I would hate for this to end in bloodshed."

"Oh, I can promise blood will be shed, but it won't be mine." My father snarled, his eyes unwavering from Niklaus, "I need to hear it from the horse's mouth: Violet, did you fuck him?"

"Dad, please," I began to sob at his side and I could see my brothers from my peripheral vision become rigid as they realized I wasn't denying my father's allegations.

"Answer me!" My father screamed, saliva flying from his lips as he spoke. "Answer me right fucking now, Violet Alannah Maddox, or I swear to the fucking lord that I will put a bullet in his skull."

"Y-Yes, it's true, but-" I cried, feeling my throat begin to close around itself.

"Leave her out of this, Maddox." Niklaus butt in, standing to meet my father's angry gaze.

"Oh, boy, you have no idea who you're fucking with," My father laughed manically."I will gut you like a pig for touching my daughter, just you fucking wait; the first thing to go will be that filthy dick between your legs."

"Dad! Please stop this!" I grabbed my father's bicep, attempting to pull him away. My father dropped his arm, but instead of controlling his emotions and sitting down to talk, I felt a crisp slap across my cheek. The blow made my head spin for a moment, my mind going blank and playing stars across my vision. Someone was quick to grab my arm and pull me away just in time for my father to be tackled to the ground. Nik straddled my father's waist, punching him in the face repeatedly as my father's head rolled from side to side with each blow.

"Don't ever fucking touch her like that again!" Nik yelled, standing slowly as my father turned on his side to stand. My mother tended to my cheek, repeatedly apologizing on my father's behalf. A pair of hands were on my waist, turning me to face him.

"Are you okay?" Niklaus questioned, his thumb running across the outline of my father's fingers on my cheek, frowning deeply as I winced at his faint touch. "Someone grab her an ice-pack." Nik demanded, to which a small woman on staff scurried off into the kitchen to avoid an further fighting. I leaned my forehead against Nik's chest and let my tears flow fluidly down my cheeks, my sobs echoing through the room because no one dared to speak. "It's going to be okay, alright? I've got you-" Niklaus gave out a strangled noise as he pulled away, my father having grabbed a fistful of Nik's curls and pulling me backward. Having full control over the younger man, my father wheeled Niklaus toward the table and slammed his forehead against the hard mahogany wood. Archor began to stand to aid his younger brother but Alphonse Hale was quick to put his hand on his eldest son's shoulder.

"You're just going to let him-"

"If roles were reversed, I would expect Talon to give me the same respect. Niklaus knew what he was doing when he engaged with the Maddox girl, he must now suffer the consequences." Alphonse sighed sorrowfully, his head hanging low. Archor grit his teeth, his eyes wide and bloodshot, feeling helpless in the room full of mobsters who were watching Talon Maddox kill his little brother. Niklaus slumped against the floor, collecting his strength and coming to his knees only for my father to deliver a punch to Nik's nose, blood splattering across my father's white button-down shirt.

"Stop it!" I cried out, reaching for Niklaus only for my mother to pull me back into the safety of her arms. My father pulled Niklaus to his feet before delivering his knee to the younger man's stomach, causing Nik to choke and crumble back down to the floor.

"This sorry sack of shit is the boy you've chosen to take your innocence, daughter?" My father laughed, grabbing my cheeks roughly with his bloodied hand. "I thought I taught you better; you've disappointed me, Violet."

"That boy gave me things I was never allowed to have at home; like freedom and choices, and the ability to make my own decisions." I cried, pulling my chin away from his grasp. "All you ever did was cage me."

"I'll show you caged, leasleanbh [little girl]. Just you wait until we get back to New York, you are never leaving your bedroom: no more painting in the gardens, no more cooking in the kitchen with your mother, no more video games with your brothers. You want to act like a poor little prisoner? Well that's what you'll be from now on." My father turned his head to look at Vaughn. "Collect the cars, we're leaving." My father grabbed my wrist and began pulling me toward the door.

"Talon, stop this, this instant!" My mother demanded, but my father acted as though no one had spoken. Vaughn got up with several of our guards and went to start the SUV's.

"No!" A voice yelled, all of us turning to see Niklaus standing up once again, his eyebrow badly cut from being punched so many times, his nose dripping blood and most likely broken. "You can't take her, she's not a twelve year old you can push around. She has the right to choose." My father dropped my hand and unbuttoned the cuffs on his sleeves, pushing them up to his elbows.

"Well, I'll give you one thing, Hale. You're not one to give up." My father turned on his heel before suddenly lunging toward Niklaus who seemed ready for the impromptu attack. Nik held out his arms and pushed my father away before elbowing him in the nose. My dad gave out a grunt of pain, but didn't let it slow him down. The two men separated and gauged each other's next possible move, my father being first to step forward throwing a punch toward Nik's stomach. Niklaus quickly moved just in time to miss the blow, but was caught off guard by my father's left hook. Nik's head flew to the side and my father ran around him, pulling him into a headlock. Niklaus gasped for oxygen as my father cut off his air supply, scratching at my father's arms in an attempt to make him let go. Nik's face began to turn purple and I couldn't stop myself from charging forward and pushing my father off of Nik. I knew that my dad could've kill Nik right there, my push would've never budged him had he not had a plan, but as I took Niklaus' head in my lap cushion it against the hardwood, my father's right-hand man, Darryl, tossed over his glock. My father cocked the gun back and I screamed.

"Stop! I'll do anything, please just stop!" I pressed my forehead against Nik's, my tears falling against his bloody skin. My father thought for a moment, his head cocking to the side.

"Alright, leasleanbh [little girl], you will go back to New York without a fight." My father stared at me, his mouth formed into a straight line. "And promise me you'll have no further contact with him ever again. No calls, no texts, no letters. It's all over here and now." My heart sunk in my chest, but really, what had I expected? I had never seen my father act this way before, but was this who he truly was? My head hung low as I gave a curt nod of acceptance. At least this way, Nik could live and find someone else to be with instead of dying tonight on my behalf. "I need to hear you say it."

"I'll go back to New York without a fight." I promised, my voice shaking with my devastation.

"And?" My father cocked an eyebrow.

"Don't do this, Malishka [baby], please." Nik said softly from my lap, a tear falling from his bruised eye. "I can't lose you."

"I won't let him kill you." I murmured, kissing his forehead lightly before looking back up at my father. "And, I promise to have no further contact with him." My father let out a sigh of relief and handed his gun back over to Darryl, holding his hand out for me to take. I gently placed Nik's head on the floor and accepted my father's invitation, standing with him to lead me out to the cars. We walked out of the dining room and toward the underground garage. My father opened the door for me and just as I was about to get in, the door to the garage slammed open.

"Violet!" Niklaus yelled, scrambling down the stairs and wincing with each step he took. Darryl and one other guard quickly apprehended Niklaus. "Get the fuck off of me! Violet! You have a choice, Malishka. Please don't go."

"This is the only way you survive this, Nik, I'm sorry." I reach for him but my father quickly catches my wrist.

"No further contact, Violet." He began ushering me inside the car and I stepped up to enter the vehicle.

"Violet!" I turned to face him once again, streams, rivers, and oceans of tears falling from my eyes as my brain began to process what was happening and what I was losing. "I love you!" He called to me, his voice breaking with helplessness.

"I love you, too, Nik." My father, having been caught off guard from my response, quickly grabbed my bicep and pulled me into the car, slamming the door shut behind me.

"Get ready Talon, that's my girl and I swear if it's the last thing I do, I'm coming for her!" Niklaus screamed as my father hopped into the driver's spot, my mother to his left in the passenger seat as we pulled away with a loud squeal from the SUV's tires. And just as my world had become bright, it was just as quickly turned back into darkness.

Chapter 23

Niklaus' lips meld against mine as his hands dip low on my back. His fingers brush across the curve of my backside until they meet the hem of my short dress. My left leg is hiked around his waist as he presses me against the nearest wall. I can feel his thick erection straining against his jeans as he grinds his pelvis into my opposite leg. His lips part from mine only to travel down my jawbone, tasting the skin of my throat as he whispers the things he is going to do to me. My core pools with sexual anticipation and I moan in approval. But suddenly, his warmth is pulled away from me. My eyes whip open in shock as I see my father straddling Nik on the floor, his hands gripping the younger man's throat. Niklaus thrashes from beneath my father, but the older man out-weighs the Hale man and Nik slowly begins to stop fighting. I throw myself on my father's back and attempt to pull him off, but suddenly I'm on the floor. Nik is nowhere to be seen but it seems I have replaced him. My father is hovering over me, his hands now on my throat.

"Daddy... What are you doing?" My lungs begin to hyperventilate as his grip becomes tighter. My hands go to grip his bicep, as if my small palms could radiate my sense of fear. "Daddy, stop, it's me Violet." My windpipe begins to close and my vision begins to blacken. My survival instincts begin to kick in and I fight, my nails digging into his skin, my legs kicking every which way in an attempt to land a blow. "Daddy, you're hurting me!" I cry out softly, my voice sounding as though I've swallowed a pound of sand and rocks.

I gasped loudly, my heart hammering in my chest just as it had in my dream. Slick perspiration dripped down my cleavage and down my back as I sat up in my bed. With my hand over my heart, I slowly stood with wobbly legs and made my way to the door. Opening it slowly, I tiptoed through the very same hall I had grown up in to find my way to the kitchen. Being in this room made me feel bittersweet. For so long, I had wished to back home in New York, and now that I was, I longed to be back home in Chicago. My now relaxed heart felt a deep urge to weep, but we had gotten past our crying phase. It had been two weeks since I had last seen Niklaus and it had been two weeks since I had last spoken to my father.

Trying to mend our broken relationship, my father had offered me a new car (as long as I never drove it myself and always had a driver with me), a small black kitten named Osiris, and the ability to take online college courses. Having accepted the last two gestures, I had spent my two weeks back at home playing with my new kitten and studying for my Gen-Ed's. But no matter how many things my father tried to buy me, nothing came close to the hole left from Nik's absence. There were times I had woken up from a light sleep at the sound of Osiris' bell, thinking it was Bear, the puppy I had left back in Chicago. There were morning I would awaken to the sound of my door opening and my heart fluttered with the excitement of seeing Niklaus, only to realize it was a maid bringing me my breakfast. All of this weighed on my mind as I tried to psycho-analyze my dream as I descended the stairs to the kitchen. Once I had entered, I blindly made my way to the fridge. Pouring myself a glass of orange juice, I felt a presence behind me and turned on my heel.

"Good morning," He said, a smirk on his face as my jaw fell slack. This man looked eerily similar to Niklaus Hale. Both of them having the same long, curly hair and similar facial hair; however, this man was an inch or two shorter with a more circular face and a more playful demeanor.

"Who the hell are you?" I questioned, placing my cup of OJ on the counter.

"I'm-"

"Liam Rolland." A familiar voice said from the kitchen door. I turned to face my father who stood with a man near his own age. "Liam, this is my daughter Violet, Violet this is-"

"Liam Rolland, yeah, I got it." I interrupted, taking a long drink from glass. "Well, nice meeting you." I attempted to head back upstairs to my room before my father caught my bicep in his hand, prompting me to stay.

"Actually, Michael and Liam are here on your account." My father said, pulling a chair out for me to sit directly across from Liam at the dining room table.

"I'm confused," I admitted, biting the inside of my cheek.

"Michael and Liam were instrumental in my pursuit to finding out information regarding the incident that sent you to Chicago. While working together, I grew to know Liam very well and he become a trusted confidant. The two of you are around the same age, so after everything that went down last week, I called Liam to see if he was available."

"Available?" I questioned, cocking an eyebrow. Feeling a great sense of unease begin to bubble in my empty stomach.

"The two of you will be formally courting starting this evening, I have made reservations for the two of you at the Rainbow Room." My father smiled, happy with the strides he was making toward giving me freedom.

"You're kidding," I said breathlessly.

"I am not, I've made reservations for the two of you at the Rainbow Room tonight-" My father said, his brow furrowing as I interrupted.

"You can't be serious! After the tantrum you threw over me and-"

"Hey, you stayed with the Hales in Chicago, didn't you?" Liam questioned, obviously trying to help alleviate the growing tension in the room. I gave a curt nod, unsure of where he was going with this. "I heard that Niklaus Hale is on a manhunt for some chick he fell in love with a couple months ago. Did you see her while you were staying there?" My heart fluttered with the prospect of Niklaus coming for me and I gave another nod.

"Something like that." I whispered softly, my head now in the clouds.

"This conversation regarding the Hales is over. Liam will meet you at the Rainbow Room at eight PM tonight, you will be dressed and on time by seven forty-five. Gentlemen." All four men rose from their seats and I stared after them in shock, both from being forced to date a man I just met at my father's arrangement and from the fact that Niklaus was looking for me.

That night, I got myself dressed in a simple pair of ripped boyfriend jeans and a loose pink sweater. As I was putting on my Vans, a guard knocked at my door in indication that it was time to leave. Each of my brothers gave me a sad, weary wave as I exited the house and hopped into the SUV that sped off down the narrow roads of New York City. When I finally arrive, the guard helped me from the vehicle and walked me inside. Liam was already waiting for me at the table and I almost felt guilty for my casual attire as he was dressed in a fine suit. Upon seeing my entrance, Liam stood from the table and pulled out my chair for me. I thanked him and sat down, but not before my eyes met with my father who was sitting with Liam's father, Michael, a few tables away. I took a deep breath, praying for some strength to get through tonight as I skimmed over the menu.

"You look beautiful," Liam noted, his own eyes skimming over the menu. Setting the menu down, I stared at him for a moment, biting the inside of my cheek. "Do you usually stare this much or should I take it as a compliment?" A blush ran over my cheeks and I shook my head.

"No, it's just... You remind me a lot of someone." I twisted an edge of the tablecloth in my hands nervously and with no interest in dating this man, I wasn't sure how this night was going to pan out. The waiter came a short time later to take our order before going back to the kitchen to deliver the ticket to the chefs. I wasn't sure what to say or even if I should get to know this man, as I doubt Niklaus was going to enjoy the idea of me on a date with another guy despite my objections to it to begin with. But Liam took charge of the conversation and asked me questions regarding my per-sonality, my likes and dislikes. After awhile our conversation dwindled into silence and I passed the time by tapping my shoes together beneath the table.

"You're not into this, are you?" Liam chuckled, running his hands through his hair.

"What?" I feigned shock, shaking my head, "No, I'm just shy." Liam rolled his eyes playfully and leaned back in his chair.

"Look, I'm not 100% feeling this either; but if I'm going to be honest with you, I overheard my father on the phone with Talon. They've made an agreement to combine our families, if it were my father's choice, we'd be tying the knot right now, but your father wanted to take things slow."

"My god," I groaned, sliding down in my chair slightly at the thought. Was there a way out of this? I mean, I was barely allowed to leave my room most days much less leave the family home, therefore, I could never run away. And even if I could get out of the house, where would I go? I have no money of my own, no car; I would have to ditch my phone so my father wouldn't be able to track me. Say everything did go well; I was able to leave the house, get away and be with Niklaus... But that meant I would never see my family again. My father would view my escape as me picking sides; the idea of not being able to see my brothers, my mother, or even my father ever again made my heart weep in my chest. I let out a deep sigh of utter frustration and Liam chuckled.

"Me too," He nodded toward the waiter who brought our food and ground fresh black peppercorn and sea salt as we desired. As we began taking our first bites, Liam's eyes flickered slightly behind us, seeing that our fathers were deep in conversation before lowering his voice. "You're the girl, aren't you?"

"I beg your pardon?" I questioned, cutting into a piece of buttery chicken breast.

"You're Niklaus' girl, aren't you?" He cocked an eyebrow, as if it were plainly obvious. My cheeks reddened and I looked away, unwilling to let the answer fall from my lips; it didn't matter anyway, Liam already knew. He smiled widely, a triumphant glint in his eyes as he took a drink to wash down his food. "That's who I remind you of, eh?" I gave a curt nod and Liam shook his head, laughing softly to himself.

"Do you know Nik?" I asked quietly, my eyes flashing to my father's as he glanced at the table. Once he looked away, Liam gave his own nod.

"I met Klaus two years ago at a Sebastian Coleman party, guy drank me under the table," Upon seeing my saddened expression, Liam frowned softly, tilting his head to the side, "You love him." A tear escaped my eyelid and I quickly wiped it away. Taking a deep breath, Liam threw back his glass of bourbon before pulling out his phone. His fingers pressed rapidly against the screen before he slipped his cell under a cloth napkin and moved it slowly toward me. With my brow furrowed in confusion, I lifted the napkin slightly and looked at the screen where a texting app was opened, the contact at the top read: Niklaus Hale.

"Liam, I can't put you in the middle of this, my father hates Nik-" I whispered, but Liam placed his index finger against his lips, signaling me to be quiet and send a message. With my heart in my ears, I discreetly took a picture of myself and sent it into the conversation. A texting bubble appeared as Niklaus typed and my heart thumped rapidly in anticipation.

What the fuck? -N

Hey there, still dressing like you're going to a funeral? -V

The phone began to ring and I felt the blood drain from my face. Liam noticed and quickly dug into his pocket, pulling out a wireless headphone.

"Stare at me as you talk so it looks like we're having a conversation, okay?" Liam instructed and I pretended to fix my hair in order to place the earbud into my left ear. With a nod, I accepted the call.

"Is this some sick fucking joke, Rolland? How the fuck did you get a picture of her?" Niklaus seethed, his voice rocking with rage.

"It's me." I said, my small sentence breaking down the middle at the sound of his voice.

"Fuck," He whispered, "Baby, fuck- Ты в порядке? Вы ударились? [Are you okay? Are you hurt?]" I laughed softly, tears filling my eyes.

"You're speaking Russian, Nik, I can't understand you." I giggled to which Liam smiled softly.

"Did he hurt you?" Nik whispered softly, "Fuck, Violet, I'm so fucking sorry for how everything went down. I swear, I planned that when my father put me in charge, I was going to sit down with your dad and do it all right, I fucked up and I'm sorry-"

"It's okay," I said softly, wishing I could be there to hug him, to comfort him. "But I have to tell you something."

"I'm going to be angry, aren't I?" He said, phrasing it like a question he knew the answer to.

"The reason I'm calling from Liam's phone is because our fathers made an agreement that our marriage would combine the Rolland and Maddox families." I said, my voice low enough that no one could here, but moving my mouth so that if my father looked over, he would think I was speaking to Liam. Niklaus' line was silent and for a moment, I thought he hung up.

"Nik-"

"Son of a fucking cock-sucker!" He yelled as several sounds of glass breaking came through the earbud. "Take my girl away from me and give her to someone else just to prove a fucking point, watch me sit down and fucking take it!"

"Nik, I don't have much more time." I warned, noting my father's eyes on the clock across the room. Niklaus took a deep breath before he continued.

"I have something to tell you, too." I could imagine him running his fingers through his hair anxiously, something he did often when he was stressed. "After you guys left, I cleaned myself up and took over; my father stepped down. I have a team of strategists in the next room throwing out ideas on how to get you back here."

"End it." Liam said quickly and I noticed my father beginning to stand.

"Nik, I have to go-"

"I love you, Violet." Nik said softly, his voice a mixture of adoration and pain.

"I love you-" The phone call ended as Liam snatched it from beneath the napkin and stuffed it back in his pocket. Our fathers approached the table, grinning down at us.

"Have fun?" Michael asked as Liam stood and reached for my hand, entwining our fingers as if we had made a miraculous love connection. I smiled up at him and nodded, my eyes meeting with my father's.

"You have no idea."

Chapter 24

"So, there's a girl?" I questioned, scanning over Liam as he smiled down at his phone. Not even bothering to glance back at me, he shoved his phone in his pocket and avoided my question. "Oh, c'mon. You know about my secret love affair, am I not entitled to know yours?"

"No, you're not." He stared ahead at the large theater screen.

"Ah, but there is a love affair!" I giggled, clapping my hands together excitedly. Liam sighed heavily, running his fingers through his hair. Glancing around at the empty theater, he leaned in slightly to whisper.

"There's a girl back home, yes, but she's been my best friend for years and I've kept my feelings to myself. She doesn't know anything about the business or the family and I intend on keeping her out of it." He gave a slight shrug as if the entire situation was fine. I gaped at him, and despite his cool outward demeanor, I knew keeping this a secret bothered him.

"She has no idea you like her?" I questioned softly, trying to get more information.

"No idea," He nodded, "I've been in love with her since middle school, but even then, I knew it would never work out. I would never want to push her into this life, I mean, I'm a trained assassin and don't make an honest living, but here I am at twenty-five years old with millions in my bank account that I can't justify for having. It kills me to see her dating, to see her live her life thinking of me as her friend. But it is what it is."

"It doesn't have to be that way-" I tried to amend, but Liam sent me a look of warning and I deflated against the back of my seat. It had been over a month since I had reconnected with Niklaus over the phone and started 'publicly dating' Liam. We had gone to the aquarium, a retro-arcade, out for a winter walk in Central Park, coffee at a small cafe in The Village, and for a ferry ride up-state. All of our dates were highly publicized due to my father's laundered business as a big-time CEO and president of Maddox Construction. An outsider's perspective on my father was one of rags-to-riches, as my father came to the United States as an immigrant from Ireland at the tender age of seventeen. Finding the love of his life and starting a family, my father built Maddox Construction from the ground up, earning me the title of heiress to a large inheritance. What outsiders didn't know was that the company was actually built with dirty money laundered from my father's underground business of assassinations, drugs, illegal weapons, and so much more. I could understand why

Liam didn't want his secret love to stay away from this life, you lived a lot longer if you lived mundanely. After the movie had finished, Liam linked arms with me and ushered me out of the theater. Our fathers waited just outside the doors, large smiles upon their faces.

"How was the show?" My father was first to speak, kissing my forehead softly.

"It was nice." I nodded, looking up at Liam in a show of adoration. Liam smiled down at me in his own act of feigned affection.

"With a date as beautiful as mine, any movie is a great one." He chuckled softly and his father clapped him on the back happily. Liam helped me into the car and the ride back to my family home was a quiet one, however, my new boyfriend had promised me a phone call with Nik as soon as we got home and my stomach tied in knots of anticipation. As he helped me out of the car, Liam smoothly placed his cell phone in my hand and I slid it up the sleeve of my shirt. Excusing myself to my bedroom to freshen up for dinner, I quickly closed the door behind me and filtered through Liam's contacts until I reached Nik's. The number rang once before he accepted the call, his voice bleeding through the quiet air.

"Malishka." He called softly, his rough voice serenading the pet-name he had assigned to me.

"Hey," I replied breathlessly, biting my lip. It had been almost a week since our last phone call and it was nice to hear his voice again. "I miss you."

"I miss you, too, baby. So much." He sighed softly. "Just a few more days, I promise you'll be back here with me."

"A few days?" My heart hammered in my chest, both with the thought of seeing Nik again and with the idea of leaving my family behind.

"Yes," I could hear the smile in his voice. "A few days. I have almost everything in order to retrieve you from New York and and baby, when I get you back in my arms, you're never leaving again." I squirmed with excitement and suddenly felt an inkling of warmth in my core. Going from having sex every single day to not having sex at all was something I hadn't been prepared for.

"I wish I were with you right now, Daddy." I whimpered softly, biting my lip a bit harder. There was a silence over Nik's end of the call before he spoke again.

"Everyone get the fuck out, I need the room." Several pairs of feet scurried their way out of the room and a door closed before Nik addressed me once again. "Does my babygirl have something to say to me?" My thighs pressed together with need and I let out a soft sigh.

"I need you." I whispered, my voice far huskier than I intend-ed.

"What do you need, babygirl?" He questioned, his voice gruff and low with arousal.

"I need your mouth on me," I fell back against the bed and ran my free hand down my body, squeezing my left breast before trailing down my navel. "I need your tongue, your fingers..."

"Where, tell me where, baby." He replied quickly, "Tell Daddy what you want from him." With a heavy blush ravaging my body, I closed my eyes and imagined he was here in my bedroom. Dipping my hand under my shirt, I gasped as my fingers found my pert left nipple, my fingertips rolled over the hardened bud.

"I need your mouth on my nipples," I said softly, imagining Nik's bountiful black curls buried between my breasts. "I want you to suck and bite them until I can't take it anymore."

"Fuck," He cursed from the other side of the phone, the clear sound of a zipper being undone sounded. I bit my lip and began kicking my jeans off, my underwear being the next article to leave my body. My hand crept between my legs and I was surprised to feel how wet I had become from mere talking over the phone with Nik. "Is my babygirl wet for me?"

"Yes!" I cried quietly, finally pressing my finger against my swollen clit, gasping at the small amount of pressure I had inflicted.

"Such a good girl, I can't wait to have you in my bed again. I want you to lay back and let me take care of you. I'll kiss every fucking inch of your body and I'll suck your nipples until they're black and blue, until you're begging me for more. And fuck, I'll give you more. I'll lick up and down that sweet pussy of yours until you force my mouth against your clit, and then I'll suck it until you're weeping for my cock." My core clenched at his words, my fingers suddenly teasing my entrance as I went along with the images behind my eyelids. "I'll line my cock up to your pussy and rub the tip against your clit while I take one of your nipples back in my mouth before fucking you relentlessly-"

A knock sounded at my door just as I pressed my fingers into my core, but my mind sobered immediately and I scrambled for my pants. Jumping into the fabric, I quickly buttoned them up and zipped my zipper just as my father entered the room. My heart hammered in my chest and I dove for the cell phone on my bed, but not fast enough that my father's eyes hadn't seen it.

"Is that a phone?" Liam and his father appeared in front of the door of my bedroom and I quickly hid the phone behind my back. "Answer me, Violet!" My father yelled. Nik's voice was screaming from the other end of the call, daring my father to speak with him. I ended the call before things could escalate. My father grabbed my arm roughly and pulled me hand out for his viewing, grabbing the phone from my palm. Noticing it was Liam's phone, his eyes narrowed as he approached the younger man.

"Did you give your phone to my daughter? I gave you strict orders that under no circumstances should she be allowed-"

"Dad, stop!" I yelled desperately, feeling tears prickle at my eyes as I realized how much worse things were going to be for me. "I stole it from him when we were at the movies." Turning to face me, my father's eyes held so much rage that I held back the urge to cower right there where I stood. But even as he took those final steps toward me, I kept my head held high.

"You have forgotten how to listen to your father," He growled lowly, his eyes darkening with his anger. "I guess I will just have to teach you, like I should have years ago."

Niklaus

The phone call ended and I stared blankly at the phone in my hand. She's in trouble, again. Would he hit her again, like he did that night? Anger rushed through my veins at the thought. My sexual frustration was gone and I was quick to pull up my boxers and pants back over my hips. Composing myself as best as I could, I opened the door to the conference room and welcomed my allies back into the room. Once everyone was seated, I leaned forward against the table.

"Fuck a few days, we leave tonight." I shouted, my voice a perfect mix between vengeance and strength. My allies looked between one another in uncertainty, but I pressed on. "Talon Maddox has taken my woman." I looked at the group of men before me. "What would you do to get back the person you love most? I realize this may mean a war, but isn't it time that Talon Maddox gets a taste of his own medicine? He was once our ally, but he has made his choice. What will yours be?" A moment of silence stretched across the conference room before

"Kheyl ili umri. [Hale or die.]" Sebastian smirked at my left, slamming his fist on the table. Each of the four most trusted men; which included Sebastian, my brother, my father, and the head of security at Hale Manor, Alec; all swore their allegiance to me and my cause. Yes, I was getting my girl back tonight, whether Talon Maddox liked it or not.

Chapter 25

V iolet

My father had shoved me into Valen's room, unsure of what to do with me. He had threatened to teach me a lesson, but after realizing Niklaus was most likely on his way to get me, he had to make a plan and quick. He took counsel with my brothers, Liam, and Liam's father, Micheal.

"We need to move Violet and her mother somewhere safe, this isn't the place for them in the middle of a war zone." Liam said as I pressed my ear to the door to listen in.

"I don't trust any of these motherfuckers anymore, after Brock and Cash, and then the Hale's , I don't know who to hand my daughter over to for her protection. Violet and her mother are completely against me on this, all I have are the people standing with me here." My father said exasperatedly. I yearned for the father I had once known and loved, I couldn't believe this is what our lives had come to.

"Maybe you should've just left her in Chicago. She was safe there-" My twin began to say quietly.

"Excuse me, son? Are you saying your little sister should be in the hands of a man who only wants her body? Who took her innocence?" My father screamed, his anger palpable even through the door.

"They seemed to love each other, I don't think he just wants sex from her." Val tried to reason.

"Violet doesn't even know what love is, she met one boy and decided to give him everything!" My father yelled and I imagined him stepping into Valen's space, trying to intimidate him.

"Who's fault is that, Dad? You've kept her here like a fucking zoo animal. She was the picture-perfect daughter for you, but she wasn't able to make friends or even have the chance to meet the opposite sex because you are too scared to let her grow up!" Viktor butt in, his voice strong and unwavering. "And instead of celebrating the fact that she bloomed into a strong woman in just months of being away from you, you tear her away from her only friend and the guy she deemed worthy enough to give her virginity to. Violet is incredibly smart and has a good head on her shoulders; she never would've fucked just any guy and I think you know that. But you couldn't control her anymore and that's what pissed you off." There was a sound of a struggle and I tried to open the door to stop them, but of course, my father had locked me in.

"Stop this! Dad, you need to wake up. Violet is nineteen years old, all of us had had sex by the time were were sixteen and you had never had a problem with us bringing girls home, hell you fucking encouraged it. But with Violet, it's the end of the world that she has a physical relationship with someone. And now you've fucked us all over." Vaughn sighed softly. "Niklaus Hale will kill us all to get to her, he won't bat an eye to it. You caught him off guard on Christmas, but he won't let that happen again."

Niklaus

The air reverberating from the Maddox family home seemed to scream luxury, wealth, and power. The Hales often kept to themselves and liked to keep their money to themselves; Maddox's... they liked to flaunt. To even get into the gate of the manor was something of a challenge, Talon having assumed I was coming for his daughter must've increased security. But what Talon didn't know was:

I was the wrong man to fuck with.

My team of over fifty men and women divided into our predetermined teams; ten of them breaching the southern gate, ten breaching the western and eastern gates and ten creating a diversion on the northern gate to create a focal point of our attack. My body vibrated with the idea of having Violet back in my arms and this time, I wouldn't let her go. My select group of ten, the most skilled fighters and strategists by my sides as we walked through the now secured southern gate.

"All clear sir." The leader of the southern group nodded to me. I clapped my hand on his shoulder in a silent symbol of thanks and began my walk to the house. Talon was undoubtedly arming his team with the best of his artillery, but I didn't have a shred of fear within my body. I was here for my woman and I was leaving here with her whether Talon lived or not. Adrenaline pumped through my every vein and my soul showered in it, ready to take on whatever was coming for me. The southern group stayed put at the gate to ensure it was secured by our team while my group of ten followed close behind me, waiting for my signal to move forward with the plan. I pressed my back against the brick wall of the Maddox house; my body, as if knowing this is the place Violet was within, took a deep breath of anticipation. There was movement from within the house and then complete silence. They were ready for us.

And just on time, the northern team shot two sets of grapple guns toward the roof of the house and all ten began climbing up. The eastern team sent round after round of bullets into the bulletproof glass windows before they came crashing down, each member then throwing a smoke bomb into their adjoining window. The western team broke into the large garage that was connected to the home and began to take over the house from within. A rainstorm of gunfire could be heard from miles away but the police wouldn't come, they knew this wasn't their business.

Taking a step back, I pulled out the glock that was resting on my hip and cocked it back, pressing the trigger as I aimed at the security system that was locking my team outside. Alarms began to blare but it only intensified my confidence. My foot collided with the door and it shot open, shards of wood flying from the sheer power of my kick. Archor threw an AK-47 over my head and I caught it mid-air before firing off into the nearest man I could see. My team spread out across the bottom floor and as soon as it was secured, I began up the stairs. My heart beat hard in my chest, my eyes scanning the hall before nodding to my team that it was safe to move forward. Suddenly, a door opened from the right and I pulled my gun up in preparation to shoot. The redhead holding his hands up in surrender smiled awkwardly at my from the doorway.

"Need some help finding her?" Valen asked, his head nodding to the right. "My dad's got her in my room, but there's a ton of armed guards including Michael Rolland, his son, and my father." Letting my gun hang loosely from my hand, I used my free opposite to shake Valen's hand in thanks and appreciation. "Well, I'm going to head downstairs and call our cleanup crew, I'm assuming there'll be a lot of dead-weights downstairs?" Val question, cocking an eyebrow. I gave a curt nod before he started toward the beginning of the stairs. Turning toward me one last time, Valen smirked softly. "You're perfect for her." And with that, he descended the stairs. Turning toward the right wing, I was unsure of whether I could trust Valen or not, but with or without his help, I would find his sister. I kicked open each door, coming up empty one after the other until I got to the final door. Taking a deep breath I kicked open the door and quickly moved to the side, several guns firing off, their target: me. I waited for the shots to stop, my team practically bouncing with the anticipation of a kill from behind me.

"Niklaus Hale, I would say, what a surprise, but it's truly not." Talon chuckled from inside the room. I slowly moved into view and my heart dropped at the sight of a lifeless Violet being held by Liam Rolland. "She's fine, just a bit faint from all the excitement." Talon continued, standing to greet me. "You've healed well since the last time we spoke."

"I'm here for Violet, I think you know that." I said sternly, my voice hard.

"You've tried my patience far more than anyone else I've ever met: first, you take my daughter's virginity before she's even married; then you threaten to keep her at the Hale Manor away from her family; and finally, you come to my home, trash the place and expect I had my only daughter over to you?" Talon laughed loudly, a smirk across Michael's face from behind him. "You're a child throwing a tantrum over his little play thing. Give it some time and you'll find someone new, but not my daughter, never my daughter." Talon raised his hand, winding it back to punch me and just as it came a few inches from my body, my palm caught the blow and I clenched my fist around his. Talon's eyes bulged in surprise and I pushed him backward, my free fist colliding with his right eye. The rest of my team entered the room and disarmed everyone, Liam stood to hand Violet over to me when Micheal pulled out a gun from his ankle holster and pulled the trigger. The bullet ripped through the skin of chest and sliced through my pectoral muscle. Archor screamed 'no' from my side and hugged my body from behind, catching me as my knees began to go slack. Another shot was fired and the second bullet penetrated my abdomen. I looked down, my body not processing the pain of my wounds, but the amount of blood seeping through my black clothing was a sign of how bad the shots really were.

"You couldn't just leave her be, now could you Hale?" Michael growled, taking a step forward as he dodge a fleet of bullets being shot at him from my team. "It was a plan, we stick to the plan." Michael beat his own fist against his chest. "The plan was simple, pay off the guards to take Violet. Collect a ransom and make it look like Liam saved the girl from an unknown party. Together they connect the Maddox and Rolland families." He beat his fist against his chest over and over before his eyes landed on Talon. "But, no, fuck the plan! You send her off to the Hale's and into the arms of Alphonse's son. Alright, fine, new plan. When Violet comes back to New York, I manipulate Talon into an arranged marriage between our children to ensure his daughter's safety, yes this will work-No, but the Hale kid came for her!" His eyes were now on me, my eyes fluttering in an out of consciousness as more and more blood left my body. Archor, with tears streaming down his cheeks, attempted to put pressure on both of my wounds. "You fuck it all up!"

"Dad..." Liam whispered, shocking by his father's revelation.

"Like you didn't know about this!" Archor screamed, his emotions running high.

"I swear I didn't, you can ask Violet, was I helping her communicate with Klaus for weeks." Liam set Violet down on the bed behind him, standing to be eye level with his father. "You set this up... So our family would have more power, more money?" Micheal's hands pressed against his son's cheeks in a lovingly sadistic moment of reason.

"It was for you, son. Everything I do is for you-"

"I don't love Violet, she belongs with Klaus, and I don't want their money or the power; I quit." Liam shoved his father away and walked out of the room, down the stairs and out of the house. Archor slapped me lightly on the cheek.

"Stay with me, Klaus, I've got you." He whispered. Violet began to ruse in her sleep, her hands and legs twitching every so often as she regained consciousness.

"Hand me my gun," I said, my voice broken from the pain that was seeping through my nerves. Archor quickly handed over my gun that I had dropped after being shot and just as

Michael aimed in an attempt to end me, I ended him. His body fell to the floor loudly even before the echo of the bullet leaving its chamber had ceased, the whole in his forehead bursting with blood.

"Niklaus, I had no idea-" Talon began to stand, his face bloodied from my fists. "I should've left her with-" I stood straight, grimacing at the pain but my eyes were only on one thing. I ignored Talon as he babbled on; I ignored the sound of Violet's brothers entering the room; I ignored my brother's pleas to 'take it easy.' I was here for her and I wasn't leaving without her. Picking her up from the soft bed, I cradled her head and the back of her knees and turned on my heel, walking out of the bedroom, down the stairs, over the dead bodies and into the waiting SUV.

Chapter 26

It had been almost four hours since we had left New York. The private flight was a little less than two and a half hours and when we had landed and drove back to Hale Manor, the first thing I made sure to do was safely place Violet in my bed. It took me twenty minutes, just sitting there looking at her, to realize I had gotten her back. I had gone several weeks without seeing this woman and I had gone mad in the process. Without her voice, without her smile... It was hard to wrap my head around her returning presence.

She's here.

There was a knock at the door and Archor popped his head in, his brow furrowed in worry. I gave a nod, knowing he was referring to my bullet wound. Pulling the door shut behind myself, Archor leaned against me and wrapped his arm around my waist.

"I'm fine." I grit, my hands involuntarily clenching onto him for support.

"The fuck you are, I don't know how you made it this long and to carry Violet all this way? Man, you've probably fucked something up in there. You couldn't set her down for a second?" He shook his head at me as we turned down the hallway to the small hospital we had within Hale Manor. It was easier having trained professionals on payroll as opposed to going to a public hospital where questions would be asked.

"No." I answered simply. He pushed open the door and helped me onto a gurney. It was a couple hours before the physician let me leave, doing x-rays to make there weren't any piece of the bullet left inside of me, pumping me with antibiotics to prevent infection, and stitching up the wound. I have a lot to do before Violet wakes up.

Violet

My head pounded softly with with a dull ache at the front of my skull. Lifting my palm to my forehead, I rubbed the sore spot in homes of relieving some of the tension. My eyes flit across the room, something familiar about it but foreign in the fact I was in my childhood home in New York. This bedroom seemed eerily close Hale Man-

My heart hammered in my chest as I made the connections in my brain. Was I truly in New York. I slid from the silky confines of the satin sheets and when my feet hit the luxury carpeted floor, my palms began to perspire with anticipation. Reaching for the door handle, I slowly turned it and peered outside. Against all reason, my sight was met with the familiar halls of Hale Manor. My naked feet padded against the floor quietly, afraid that if I made a noise, I would wake up from this dream. It had to be a dream. I wanted to find Nik, I needed to find him. I needed to tell him I loved him and I missed him, even if this was all a figment of my imagination. Turning the corner to the hallway that lead to my old bedroom, I let my fingers trail down the walls, remembering my first day at Hale Manor.

"I'm nineteen, not nine and I may be spoiled but I'm thankful for everything I have. I don't know what I did to offend you, but I do not deserve this!" I folded my arms across my chest. He was quiet for a moment before he slammed me against the wall, his warm breath fanned over my lips as he spoke.

"Little girl, do not push me." He laughed manically, "I may be in charge of keeping you safe, but I can make anything look like an accident."

My cheeks reddened at the remembrance of how embarrassingly turned on I was by Niklaus, even with his open threat floating in the air. My fingertips slipped across the keypad that allowed access into my room and the door's pressurized system lifted, opening the steel door for my entrance. Slipping into the room, the first thing I noted was that it was dimly lit throughout, the lights were not on but instead hundreds of candles lined the floor and furniture of my bedroom. Rose petals were sprinkled across the floor, along my vanity, dresser and bed, however right in the middle of the room, red petals were formed into four words.

Will you marry me?

Tears welled in my eyes as a figure moved from inside the walk-in closet, his body clad with a black suit, black tie, and shiny black shoes. His hair was just as curly and untamed as when I left him last, is lips tipped in a soft smile. His hands holding a single red rose.

"Hey there, little troublemaker." He smirked, taking a few steps forward so there was only a mere foot between us. "I have been punched, kicked, stabbed and shot; I've been threatened, held hostage and tortured. But nothing, and I mean absolutely nothing, has hurt me more than losing you." He closed the space between us, cupping my cheek in his free hand. "So give me the chance to keep you." Ghosting a light kiss on my lips, Niklaus bent down on one knee and pulled out a small black box before pulling it open and revealing a beautiful ring. "With the ring that was passed down from my grandmother to my mother, I ask you, Violet Alannah Maddox, to be my wife." Tears fell freely down my reddened cheeks, each choked breath being caught in my throat.

"Yes." I whispered, nodding softly with a smile growing on my lips. "Yes!" Nik grinned and threw his arms around my waist, lifting me up in the air and spinning me around happily. Slowly loosening his grip, I slid down the length of Nik's body and when our faces were level, he caught my lips with his own.

"Thank you," He murmured between kisses, repeating the two words over and over as he kissed me deeper, each one growing more in passion. I slipped my fingers around his torso and pulled his tucked in shirt from his pants, unbuttoning each button from his black dress shirt until it hung unceremoniously from his shoulders from beneath his jacket. Shrugging both articles of clothing off, I tore his black tank top from his body and threw it somewhere in the room, my fingers tracing the lines of his muscles down to his happy trail. Placing kisses on his warm skin, my fingers worked at his belt and pants, both falling to the floor with a soft thump. Realizing I was fully clothed, Nik eagerly pulled my long sleeved crop top away from my body and tore away my bra, the fabric making an audible rip as the discarded it on the floor.

"Hey-" I giggled, feeling my nipples pebble from the sudden rush cool air.

"I'll buy you a new one." He growled softly, unbuttoning my skinny jeans before ridding me of both the Levi's and my panties. Throwing me over his shoulder, Nik turned on his heel and threw me onto the bed before crawling on as well, his tongue licking a stripe up from my ankle to my lips before ravishing my mouth. I moaned into the sloppy kiss, my fingers becoming lost in his curls as his tongue battled against mine. Whining softly as he pulled away, I looked down at Niklaus as he pulled my left nipple into this mouth, rolling the hardened nub repeatedly against his tongue. I arched my back, my body begging for more and Nik quickly obliged, leaving my left nipple for my right while his fingers trailed down my navel. He played with the slight tuft of red hair that had grown in the absence of a razor while I had been living back in New York with my family and I blushed in embarrassment. Noticing this, Nik quickly pecked my lips.

"You're so fucking beautiful, Violet." He whispered, leaving a trail of kisses down my throat before finding his way to my heat. Wasting no time, his tongue was quick to find my clit and I writhed from beneath him. My hips bucked against his mouth and he forced them down with his free hand while his other began to play at my entrance. His fingers slid between my folds and I threw my head back, crying out in a pleasure I hadn't experienced in weeks. "That's right, baby girl, who's making you feel good?"

"You, Daddy!" I whimpered, pressing my hips firmly against his finger so he was knuckle deep within me. He groaned at the sight, taking a deep breath as he watched me come undone.

"Don't you come, Malishka, you will not come until my cock is buried inside that tight pussy of yours, is that understood." He questioned and I nodded quickly, needing him to take me now. Kicking off his boxers, Niklaus positioned himself between my thighs. "Look at me, Violet." When our eyes met, he pressed is thumb against my lower lip, pulling at it slightly. "You will be my wife."

"I will be your wife." I repeated softly, a smile growing on my lips despite the burn in my core.

"Your name will be Violet Hale." He pressed the tip of his member into my entrance and my eyes began to roll in the back of my head. My heart thumped hard in my chest at his words. Violet Hale. "And I will love you forever." Suddenly, Nik plunged deep within me, sending me over the edge, clenching around his large manhood in a vice-like grip. Groaning from the pressure of my womanhood, Nik slowly pulled out and pressed back in. He was making love to me. Nik peppered my collarbones with kisses, kissing my swollen lips each time I came for him. The entire day consisted of making love, taking a bath together, eating chocolate strawberries and making love again. It was hard not to continue to fall further in love with him, more so than I thought to be possible.

The next day, Niklaus was able to keep his touches to a minimum for us to leave the bedroom. He gathered everyone in the Hale family into the dining hall, insisting that we all sat down for a meal together now that I was home. Alphonse was sitting happily next to his son who had proved himself to be a strong leader, Archor sitting on the other side of his father with an expression of relief. All was well again.

"Attention," Niklaus said at the head of the table, "I have gathered you all here to share great news." With a long theatric pause, he grinned down at me, "I've asked Violet to marry me and she said yes." The room erupted into an assemblage of clapping, hoots and hollers. Nik kissed me forehead before regaining his seat beside me. Alphonse smiled widely across from me, giving me a nod of what I interpreted to be his blessing. I looked around the room, a bright smile on my own face as I came to terms with my life being completely backward from what it had been a year ago. I had been a sheltered daughter to man who wouldn't let me grow up and it was because of my father's business that my life had been put in danger. But as my eyes found that of my fiancee... I knew that every bit of it was worth it. My mafia babysitter turned out to be my knight in shining armor. What a better ending to a fairytale than that? The knight saved the princess not only from the monsters outside her castle walls, but those within as well. Niklaus placed his hand on mine, noticing I had drifted off in thought.

"Are you okay, Malishka?" He asked softly, his thumb coming out to graze over my knuckles.

"Yes," I nodded gently before feeling a suddenly shift within my belly. My eyebrows shot up in surprise and Nik watched me in confusion. A wave of nausea flooded my senses and I covered my mouth, running to the nearest bathroom. The door clicked open and a familiar hand rubbed my back softly.

"I don't know how many times I told you to make him wear a condom, babydoll." Ravon handed me a towel to wipe my mouth and I quickly rid the excess vomit from my lips before tumbling him to the ground in a hug.

"I missed you!" I squealed, resting my head on his shoulder as he chuckled and embraced my affections.

"I missed you more, girl." He pulled away, taking my hands in his. "But it seems like you came back with more than what you left with." His eyes ventured to my belly and the blood drained from my face.

"You don't thin-"

"Oh honey baby, I know. I knew right away when I saw you; your boobs and ass are bigger, and it explains why you've been so tired lately." He helped me to my feet.

"How did you know I've been tired? I've been gone for weeks-"

"Liam and I go way back, everybody knows everybody, Violet. He happened to let it slip you'd been sleeping quite often, eating more. He chalked it up to depression, but I know how often you and Nik got freaky, it doesn't take a scientist, girl." He smirked softly. Nik burst into the bathroom, cupping my cheeks.

"What's wrong, baby, are you sick?" He questioned worriedly. Ravon and I exchanged a look before bit my lip softly.

"You're gonna want to sit down for this."

Epilogue

A beautiful, rich smell drifted through the kitchen of Hale Manor. My hand clenched around the handle of the oven and pulled the door open, my opposite oven mitt-clad hand pulled out the cake responsible for such a delicious aroma. Placing the cake pan on a safe surface, I flipped it over onto a plate and watched the decadent baked good slide from the metal pan. As I waited for the cake to cool, I exited the kitchen and put the finishing touches on the decorations in the dining hall. Rose gold and silver streamers lined the beautiful, dark dining hall; the dining hall I had eaten my meals in for a little over twenty years. I passed a mirror as I dumped more ice into the several different kinds of punch we had set up for the guests.

My red hair had a few stray strands of silver hair peaking through, and a few wrinkles had formed at the crinkle of my eyes and around the smile lines of my lips; but I mostly looked the same. Sure, I was almost forty, but I still got it. A small redheaded boy burst through the door to the dining hall, dressed in the little tux I had laid out on his bed earlier in the afternoon.

"Mom, I can't find my other shoe!" My youngest sighed in frustration. I rolled my eyes playfully and twirled him around toward the door.

"Dmitri, please go ask Uncle Ravon to help you, I've got lot to do before your sister's party." Patting the ten-year-old's bottom, I shooed him out of dining hall and made my way back into the kitchen. Now cooled, the cake waited patiently for me to frost it with the rich buttercream frosting I had prepared earlier. After forty-five minutes, I stood back to look at the finished product, my eyes gleaming with an unspoken pride. A large pair of rough, calloused hands wrapped around my waist, a chin slipping into the nape of my neck.

"My love, my light, my wife..." He murmured softly in my ear, kissing a trail up my jawline. "Twenty years has gone by and you are just as delectable as the day I first saw you."

"You didn't like me when you first met me though," I cocked an eyebrow, a small smile playing on my lips.

"Yes, well, I still thought you were hot." Nik spun me around to face him, my red hair swirling around with the sudden movement. I giggled softly, placing my hands upon his broad chest as he leaned in to kiss me. He was right, twenty years had gone by but our spark had done anything but dwindle. Our lips moved fervently, both trying to gain dominance without much success. Grabbing a fistful of my hair, Nik pulled me closer as my hands traveled down and slipped into his pants, squeezing his plump backside. Chuckling against my mouth, he went to lift me up and set me onto the counter but I squealed in protest. "What?"

"Um, your daughter's cake?" I turned around and pointed to the cake with an expression of obviousness. Niklaus leaned against the counter and stared at the cake for a long time, his face unreadable as he silently stood like a statue. "Babe, what's wrong?" My fingers splayed out against his back, gently running my hands up and down the length of his spine.

"She's twenty." He said softly, his eyes distant.

"Yes," I nodded, feeling myself as that time had passed far too quickly.

"Violet, she's leaving." He sighed softly, lost within his own thoughts. "I don't understand why the university here isn't good enough."

"She's spent her entire life here and put in two years at Columbia, she wants to explore, can you blame her?" I questioned, feeling him tense beside me.

"No," He ground out, "But why does she have to go so far?"

"She will visit and besides, Vivian will take good care of her in California, I have complete faith in my cousin to watch over. Besides, Griffin is going to the same school so she'll have at least one familiar face and Viv's brother-in-law is a cop, how much trouble can she really get into?" I smiled softly despite my heavy heart. My first child was about to move across the country, I wanted her to be happy and live her life, however that didn't stop the empty feeling of letting her go. The door to the kitchen suddenly opened and one of the guards popped their head in.

"Mrs. Hale," He nodded toward me in respect, "Klaus, Sebastian and Griffin Coleman are here for the party." Nik gave a nod and took my hand in his, leading the way to greet our guests. When we entered the main hall, I smiled at my long time friend, greeting him with a tight hug.

"Bash! How've you been?" I pulled away, allowing Sebastian and Nik to shake hands with big, matching grins.

"Not bad, not bad. I just finished up helping this guy pack for college!" Sebastian punched his son in the shoulder and they both laughed. My eyes traveled to the tall young man before me, his hair messy yet, seemingly put together; apart from his hazel eyes, he looked like a carbon copy of his father with dirty blonde hair, a tall and slender body but not without tone, clad with a fitted navy blue suit and black tie underneath; a five o'clock shadow had formed on his cheeks, upper lip, and chin. His eyes swept past me down the hallway, searching for something he couldn't find.

"Are you excited for the move?" I questioned Griffin softly, his eyes readjusting and focusing on me. He smiled smoothly, a dimple imprinting on his cheek. This dimpled smile brought me back to the night Griffin was found, just a bundle one year old standing outside of Sebastian's house in uptown New

York. Sebastian had opened the door having heard something from outside and having assumed it to be a pizza delivery man, he opened it with a wad of cash in hand. A wail had sounded and Bash couldn't believe his eyes, the toddler looked up at him with large beaded tears falling down his cheeks. A long letter, including a legal document declaring both Sebastian's paternity and the mother's withdrawal of rights to their child had been pinned to young Griffin's coat. Because Bash had had so many sexual partners, it was hard to narrow a search to find Griffin's mother and after two years of searching, Sebastian gave up and raised Griffin alone.

"Of course, I mean, Dad and I have been to California plenty of times, so I'm no stranger to the area, but college will be a whole new playing field." Griffin stuffed his hands in his pockets; cool, calm and collected. "But I'm ready to go to school now that I've taken a couple years off to travel."

"So where is my god-daughter?" Bash questioned, looking around at the decorated walls.

"She's in her room getting ready-" Nik started as the doorbell rang once again. People began flooding through our doors and into the dining hall, all ready to be apart of our daughter's twentieth birthday celebration.

Third Person

It was eight o' clock and the guests had all arrived. Every Hale and Maddox in the country had come for the joyous event, yes, even grandfather Talon. It was remarkable to see the mended relationship between Mister and Missus Hale and Talon Maddox, it had taken years, but they had become a family. Alphonse Hale took up conversation with his old friend while the rest of the guest waited in anticipation, many of them having not seen the eldest daughter of the Hale's since she was in infancy.

Niklaus Hale's foot tapped against the floor, his eyes glancing at his watch for the seventh time. Where was she? He shot a questioning look to his wife and she gave a shrug. Moving toward the door, Sebastian and Talon followed behind him; the father, godfather, and grandfather all curious as to where the birthday girl had run off to. They turned the corner and Nik gave a quick knock to his daughter's door.

"Sapphire, love, are you ready-" Niklaus stopped mid-sentence upon realizing her room was empty. With a heavy sigh, he shook his head at his comrades and continued down the hall. They searched room after room, coming up short with nothing but maids. Niklaus was becoming frustrated.

Where the hell was she?

"Uh, Klaus..." Sebastian nodded toward the poolroom, the glass door fogged so much that sight into the room was limited to an opaque film. Niklaus grabbed the handle to the door and whipped it open, quietly stepping into the poolroom. His eyes scanned the room until he found what he had been looking for. His jaw fell slack in shock, the godfather and grandfather having similar expressions on their faces.

Pressed against the poolroom wall was Sapphire Hale, her deep red hair splayed wildly around her shoulders as she lost herself in a deep, frenzied kiss. Her eyes closed and her entire being oblivious to her father's presence in the room. A hand that didn't belong to his daughter slid down her waist and grabbed her backside. Niklaus recognized that dirty blonde hair. Suddenly, Niklaus' fists balled at his sides and all he could see was red, a target surrounding the messy tousled hair of the Coleman offspring.

"Griffin!" Niklaus seethed, a hand clapping on his shoulder from behind. Talon Maddox smiled wickedly, feeling a glorious bout of satisfying irony. The young couple tore apart from each other, Sapphire's suddenly reddened cheeks visible now that she wasn't sucking face with her father's best friend's son.

"Dad," She whispered, horrified and embarrassed, "Please, let me explain-"

"Yes, please explain why Griffin Coleman's tongue was down your throat." The father seethed, his anger flushing his system.

"Klaus," Griffin stood in front of Sapphire, as if to protect her from something, "Don't be upset with Sapph, this is on me-"

"It would be in your best interest to shut your fucking mouth." Niklaus growled, a million ways to murder the boy running through his head. Griffin looked to his father for help, whom just merely shrugged. Sebastian had told Griffin not to pursue the Hale girl, the father merely giving his son an 'I-told-you-so' look. Talon Maddox squeezed Niklaus' shoulder, leaning in close to the younger man's ear to whisper.

"Karma's a bitch, isn't it?" And with that, Talon left the room, allowing the Hale man decide for himself what he was to do. A father loves his daughter and now Niklaus had to pay the price of such a love, just as Talon had. As he walked down the hallway back to the dining hall, Talon thought about the story he had once told Violet when she was a girl, coming to terms with how the story had come full circle.

The old king had been wrong to keep the princess locked away, away from the danger he had thought was lurking outside the castle. He had become possessive of her and had learned his lesson the hard way. The princess became a queen and had her own little princess, however, the new King, King Niklaus, would quickly find out that princesses are hard to let go of.

When Talon reentered the dining hall, he pulled his daughter into his arms with a bone crushing hug. He was proud of whom his princess had become, even despite his mistakes as a parent. She smiled up at him and he couldn't help but think...

The had lived happily ever after.

www.ingramcontent.com/pod-product-compliance
Lightning Source LLC
Chambersburg PA
CBHW070940190726
48292CB00004B/1269